S

10/20

THE TRUTH PROJECT

DANTE MEDEMA

Quill Tree Books
An Imprint of HarperCollins Publishers

Quill Tree Books is an imprint of HarperCollins Publishers.

The Truth Project
Copyright © 2020 by Dante Medema
All rights reserved. Printed in the United States of America. No part of this
book may be used or reproduced in any manner whatsoever without written
permission except in the case of brief quotations embodied in critical articles and
reviews. For information address HarperCollins Children's Books, a division of
HarperCollins Publishers, 195 Broadway, New York, NY 10007.
www.epicreads.com

Library of Congress Control Number: 2020937189
ISBN 978-0-06-295440-4

20 21 22 23 24 PC/LSCH 10 9 8 7 6 5 4 3 2 1
❖
First Edition

To Bug. My first baby. My always sister.

THE
TRUTH
PROJECT

My parents created everything in the image
of a perfect Alaskan family.

The home on the hillside
a cabin in Kenai
2.5 kids
matching Xtratuf boots
a 5-star safety-test-rated Volvo
with all-wheel drive.

Pretty sure I'm the .5 kid.

Sana-Friend ♥

Sana: You know what I think?

Me: It's awfully late to be texting?

Maybe I should let people sleep?

Maybe I should BE asleep?

Sana: You're not people.

You're my Cordelia.

Me: What do you want?

Sana: She's grumpy when she's tired.

What are you going to do when you go off to fancy AF Columbia University and have to stay up all night going to frat parties so you can fit in?

Me: I might be up late, but I am not going to frat parties.

Sana: You're no fun. Did you submit your senior project proposal yet?

Me: No, I thought I'd wait until the last minute.

Sana: . . .

Me: Obviously a joke. I turned it in the first day submissions were open.

Sana: See? This is why Columbia gave you early acceptance.

Did you remember to request me as a partner?

Sorry to hound you again but I'm nervous. I really need a good partner.

You know I choke when it comes to written stuff.

Me: Yes, I remembered. You're going to do fine even if we don't get paired.

Sana: Easy for you to say. You're like really good at school stuff.

Even if I GET into college I'm going to need a good grade on my senior project to keep my GPA up.

Me: Oh my gosh. Stop!

Sana: You barely need to try. So you can focus all your energy on helping me record some soccer lessons. And edit them. And share them on all your social media. And maybe do the entire written portion for me?

K. Thanx.

Me: Hey. I have to try. Just like anyone else.

I already ordered the GeneQuest kit.

Any day now I'll be researching my ancestry and writing poems about it.

Plus it's going to tell me adopted.

Sana: Here we go

Me: What?

Sana: Always with the "I'm adopted" and "I don't fit in."

I get it. You don't feel like you fit in, but you're not fucking adopted.

You have the best life.

Don't shit on it.

I'd trade my trailer for your hillside mansion any day.

Me: For the last time, it's not a mansion.

I love your trailer. It's cozy, and no one walks into your room without knocking.

Sana: That's because I don't have a room.

GOD Delia! Way to make me feel bad about my life!

Me: . . .

I'm sorry. You know that's not what I meant.

Sana: . . .

Me: Sana.

Sana: I know.

But it's still kinda like a shelter dog listening to a forever-home dog complain about his living arrangements.

I'll also take extra help on my college application. Thanks.

Pretty soon you'll be off at Columbia living the life.

While I'm stuck here in Tundra Cove.

Me and my soccer ball.

The sign entering town says:
Tundra Cove
Population 5,356
If we don't already know you, we will.

Sana always says there's nothing to do here.
That it's the same parties
with the same people
trying to prove
you don't know them
as well as you think.

I always thought I could spend my whole life here.
Finding beauty in the small things.
The way we're nestled close enough to the inlet
that you can see beluga whales breach
or watch blue melt into pink in a perfect
cotton candy sunset over the water.
But also we're on a mountain,
with endless trails to get lost on
and giant trees that seem to shoot up
out of nowhere
so high I forget
that the leaves at the top
aren't part of the sky.

But Sana has always been too big for this town.
She needs to tell people they don't really see her
—prove them wrong.
I don't tell them I'm different,
because why bother?
They'd never believe me anyway.

To: Cordelia Koenig (koenig.cordelia@tchs.edu)
From: Vidya Nadeer (nadeer.vidya@tchs.edu)
Subject: Re: Senior Project Application

Cordelia,

I'm so glad to get your proposal! I adore the idea of using a GeneQuest DNA kit to discover your roots and find how ancestry shapes you as a person through poems. I've lived in Tundra Cove since I was a child, but my family is from Kashmir with entirely different traditions and customs.

I like this idea—I do—however I can't help but notice (despite the poetry aspect) you chose the exact same project as your older sister, Beatrice. I was her advisor as well, and while I expect you will impress me equally with yours, I want to ensure you take a great deal of effort to make this your own. Sometimes students with early acceptance can skim through the rest of their senior year, and I want you to get the most out of it. This grade is still very important to your GPA. Please let me know how you intend to make this stand out from Beatrice's.

I've assigned Kodiak Jones as your partner. I agree with your email: the two of you will work well together, and hopefully I can convince both of you to join me next month for the Pacific Northwest Young Poets Conference. As I mentioned in class, I will be speaking there and taking a group of promising students. Please consider attending.

That's all I have for now,

Vidya Nadeer

I can never tell Sana the truth.
How before she asked me to request her,
I'd already requested Kodiak Jones.

Because when he performed
at the slam poetry contest last year,
he broke apart, free like the bald eagles
who live near the inlet.

His arms spread into wings,
the vibration in his chest
daring our school to judge him.

When Kodiak almost sang his words,
like it was the only way to let them out—
a soft rhythm
followed by a crescendo
I felt them in my soul.

Because he's not the silly boy
I told ghost stories with.
The boy I grew up admiring.
He's the boy who staples
pages of his notebook shut
like even he's afraid to see
what's between them.

Whose brown eyes dart away
if I let myself look too long.
The boy who sings his poetry
the way I can only dream to do.

Dinner is always the same.

My sister, Iris, speaks in hashtags
because she's twelve and thinks it's funny.
She puts up air quotes. Hashtag Boring. Hashtag Tired
Hashtag I-don't-want-to-go-to-school-anymore.
Hashtag can't-it-be-summer-so-I-can-be-outside?

Dad speaks in Shakespeare
because he's a professor and thinks it's funny.
His day was quiet.
He's grading papers for Lit 101.
He's got some promising students this year.

Mom rolls her eyes at them both
because she's a real estate agent
and doesn't think anything is funny.
She has a new listing she can't wait to sell.
Maybe this is the one that'll make her stop working so
hard.
That will make her smile instead of frown at the phone
she's glued to.

I clear my throat, and they all stare.

Because I get lost in metaphors they don't understand.
My stories live in daydreams
written in verse
I never, ever share.
Unfit for lighthearted dinner conversation.

Every. Single. Night.

"My day was good," I say.
"We got our project partner assignments."
They wait, and I see Mama crumple a little bit when I say,
"Kodiak Jones."

Mom's face twists like it's sour,
but I know it's not the wine.
She's friends with Kodiak's mom.
Both real estate agents,
same church,
play on the same recreational softball team.
They share secrets like they share recipes.

Dad doesn't care about Kodiak.
"What did you decide on for your project?"
"Poetry, that's wonderful—can I help?"
But he teaches Shakespeare, not poetry.
"'It is a wise father that knows his own child'—
William was a poet!"
He jokes.
He quotes.
He always jokes and quotes.

"Be careful,"
Mama says.
"That boy is trouble."

Who is this boy you see?
Kodiak isn't trouble.
He's troubled.

Before he was "trouble" he was
"Kodiak."

And he was the boy I spent every Tundra Cove summer
following around on my bike with skinned knees
and terrible tan lines where my shorts met my thighs.

The one whose family used to go to the fair with us
—a 2-hour drive—every year.
And our parents would walk around
while we ate corn on the cob
and rode the Tilt-A-Whirl until we felt sick.

He was the same boy who taught me how to whistle.
And when his mouth curled around like a little O
I felt my heart skip a beat for the first time.
The person I shared my first poem with.
And it was okay,
because he was sharing poems with me too.
Kodiak was my best friend
before I even knew who Sana was.

And one day
on our way home from school,
kicking stones down a muddy path

under giant spruce trees,
I told him about my first crush.

That my stomach felt a little funny
whenever he was around.
And that I played out entire conversations
with him in my head,
wondering if I'd ever have the courage
to tell him out loud
what I felt in my heart.

Kodiak never smiled
and never teased.
And I never said
I was talking about him.

It happened slowly.
First he stopped walking home with me
to hang out in the woods behind the school.
That's where he started smoking.
And one day when I walked back
to where trees protected the gnarled roots
from snow—
they were all gathered around a pit
with empty cans and trash everywhere.

I asked him why.
He told me,
"Sometimes you do things you don't understand
to make sense of the things you do."
But he wasn't looking at me.

He was looking at *her*.
Liv. The new girl with a wild smile and purple hair.
And once he was Liv's, he wasn't anyone else's anymore.
He looked at her
the way I always wanted him to look at me
and they kissed
the way I wanted to kiss him.

When his mom sat at our kitchen table crying
because she walked in on them in his room,

she said she didn't know
what to do with him anymore.
She found cigarettes and vodka and
at-least-they-were-being-safe condoms.
He was skipping school.
He wasn't coming home.
And in the hallways,
when I'd wave,
he didn't look at me
like a boy I ever knew.

I thought maybe we'd lost him for always.
But then everything last year happened
and he changed again.

Then when I saw him in the hallways
he started smiling again
like maybe he had made sense of what
he didn't understand before.

Sana-Friend ♥

Sana: Deeeeeelia

Deeeeelia!

CORDELIA ANN KOENIG ANSWER MY TEXT
RIGHT NOW

Me: You know my middle name isn't actually Ann, right?

Sana: Bullshit.

Me: What do you need, friend of mine who can't let me
eat dinner without blowing up my phone?

Sana: I just got an email from my new advisor. They
switched me to Mr. Kim.

So racist. I bet I got paired with him since he's Asian AF
and I'm half Asian AF.

Me: Well, Ms. Nadeer is Indian and I'm white AF, so
there goes that theory.

Sana: I had Ms. Nadeer! That's what I don't get. All of a
sudden they switch me to Mr. Kim and I got paired with
Madison Lee. See where I'm going with this?

Me: This doesn't have anything to do with the fact that
you and Maddy basically run the soccer team and both
your senior projects involve soccer, plus Mr. Kim happens
to be the coach?

Sana: Plus they didn't pair me and you as project
partners which is STUPID. Literally everyone else I know
who made requests got them.

Me: I know! I got my letter too!

I had Honors English with Maddy sophomore year. She'll be great at helping you with the written portion.

Sana: You're still going to help me record some soccer lessons right?

Me: Find a student yet?

Sana: Yeah! There's a girl three trailers down who wants me to teach her. Her mom told me she'll pay in cigarettes so that's cool.

Me: That's perfect! Starting your prison money stash early, I see.

Sana: Who'd you get paired with?

Me: I'm afraid to tell you.

Sana: Shut up. It better not be Emma. If it's Emma Daniels I'm going to scream.

Me: . . .

Sana: Oh my fucking stars. It's Emma Daniels. Can you please ask her if she's gay?

Or bi?

Please let her be at least a little bi.

Me: Why don't you use your internet sleuthing skills to figure that out?

Spoiler alert.

It's not Emma

Sana: As if I haven't tried. Can you still ask her?

Me: Staaaaaaahp! I am not going to ask her if she's gay.

Sana: C'mon. I've only liked her since ninth grade.

Me: Back when you were still pretending to like boys.

Sana: Yes. Think of the heartache Emma could have saved Liam.

Me: Poor Liam.

Sana: May he rest in peace.

Me: He's not dead!

Sana: He is to me! He did not react well at all to me coming out.

Me: In his defense you did lie to him about being straight for like a year.

Sana: Meh.

So really.

Who'd you get set up with?

Me: Kodiak Jones.

Sana: Shut the front door. Kodiak?

I can't believe someone even got paired with him after last year.

Huh.

He's an odd fit for you don't you think?

Little miss perfect poet who never breaks the rules and . . . ?

How do you describe the train wreck that was last year?

Me: It makes a lot of sense, actually. His project also involves poetry.

Sana: Still. How did that happen?

Me: No idea.

Sana: He won't need any help. He probably won't even do the project.

I heard he's missed so much school he's going to repeat next year anyway.

So you can still help me fail at mine.

While you're at college next year I can work at the world's last Blockbuster and use up all those cigarettes my neighbor promised.

Me: You're going to college.

I read over all your applications.

They were solid.

Stop worrying.

Sana: The Sasaki women aren't known for college-going.

Me: . . .

Sana: Okay fine. I never got to meet anyone from my dad's side of the family.

I have no idea what the Sasaki women are known for.

But going off my mom's side I'm more likely to get pregnant in six months.

Me: Pretty hard to get pregnant when you only want to do girls.

Sana: Touché.

To: Vidya Nadeer (nadeer.vidya@tchs.edu)
From: Cordelia Koenig (koenig.cordelia@tchs.edu)
Subject: Re: Re: Senior Project Application

Dear Ms. Nadeer,

Thank you so much for your input. As you might remember, I was incredibly inspired during your poetry unit in AP English last semester. Since, I've made it my goal to implement poetry into my life in as many ways as I can before going to Columbia this fall. I intend to use poetry as my primary form of exposition for my senior project as I discover how my genealogy affects me personally. I know Beatrice found her look into our ancestry to be life changing, and I can only hope this project will help me grow as a poet while I learn something new in the process.

I have already sent out my GeneQuest kit, with DNA swab, and their lab should be sending my results any day now. Instead of relying on Bea's results, which I'm told can differ even between siblings, I have taken initiative to make this project my very own.

Sincerely,

Cordelia

To: Cordelia Koenig (CordeliaBedelia99@gmail.com)
From: K. Jones (therealkodiakjones@gmail.com)
Subject: senior project partners FTW

Cordelia! What up?!

Funny. I got my email from Ms. Nadeer that we're partners. I was trying to find your email address and came across some of our old chats from way back in the day. Mostly dumb stuff, but I found one from the end of 8th grade—old school. Remember when we went on the field trip to the zoo and got lost near the wolf exhibit and I convinced you they open the enclosure at night? The look on your face when they started howling. Good times.

Pretty cool we got paired up as partners for our projects. Should we meet up tomorrow after school and talk? I can come over if that works. Figure out how we can help each other?

Kodi

Ps. My mom says hi.

Pps. Wait—this is still your email, right?

Hey new number, who dis?

Kidding. I'll rock the Cordelia Bedelia email until I die. Same with my treasured copy of Amelia Bedelia in hard print.

First of all, I'm glad you have fond memories of that day, but I legit thought I was going to die. Let's start with the fact that you said if we were exposed to man-eating wolves, you would survive because you could run faster. Not cool. At all.

It's kinda crazy to think back to then. Before high school. I can't believe we used to walk home together every day, and now I can't remember the last time we talked. I miss hanging out in your parents' backyard, roasting marshmallows and telling scary stories. Your dad always told the best ones.

But yeah, it's awesome we're partners. Tomorrow sounds good!

Cordelia Bedelia.

Ps. Tell your mom I said hi back.

It's late
when Mom comes in,
and I have just enough time
to close my laptop.

She drops laundry on my bed,
then drapes her hand
on my shoulder.

"Why don't you like Kodiak?"
I ask.

Mom softens,
threading her fingers through
the ends
of my too-curly hair.

"It's not that I don't like him,"
she says.
"But I wouldn't be a good parent
if I didn't try to prevent you
from making the same mistakes
as your mother."

When I don't try to argue
she leaves me alone,

and I fire my email back up
hoping
praying
he's already written back.

Sometimes I wonder what mistakes
she sees in herself
that she's afraid to see in me.

To: Cordelia Koenig (CordeliaBedelia99@gmail.com)
From: GeneQuest (donotreply@genequest.com)

We have your results!

Click here to see where you come from!

Deep down, I know what it will say.

I'm not so different.
Them
and
me.

Deep down I know
I'm looking for confirmation
that
there
is
a
reason
I
don't
fit.

My Results

61.1% British & Irish

22.2% French & German

13.8% Broadly Northwestern European

1.4% Southern European

1.1% Broadly European

0.3% Nigerian

0.1% Broadly Western Asian & North African

To: Cordelia Koenig (CordeliaBedelia99@gmail.com)
From: GeneQuest (donotreply@genequest.com)

You have new

GeneQuest relatives!

Click <u>here</u> to connect to your DNA family!

(If you can't see relatives, make sure you've got "search

function" set to ON in settings)

GeneQuest

Start connecting with your family!

Name	Relationship
Jack Bisset	**Father**

Father's side. 50% DNA shared.
99.9% accurate

It doesn't matter that others are listed.
an uncle—25% shared DNA
a grandmother—25% shared DNA
a cousin—12.5% shared DNA

I can't see past Father.
Jack Bisset—50% shared DNA.

As if this is common knowledge
that somewhere a man lives
who genetically
is my father.

I can't stop staring outside
to a light snow
inching up my windowsill,
creating a blanket between me
and the world.

I slide down in my bed
hugging a pillow
and repeating over and over and over and over again.

I was right. I. Am. Adopted.

I was right. I. Am. Adopted.

I was right. I. Am. Adopted.

I was right. I. Am. Adopted.

I was right. I. Am. Adopted.

I was right. I. Am. Adopted.

I was right. I. Am. Adopted.

I was right. I. Am. Adopted.

I was right. I. Am. **Adopted.**

Sana-Friend ♥

Me: I'm freaking out.

Sana: Too much Taco Bell?

Me too friend.

Me. Too.

Me: No, this is serious.

I just got the GeneQuest results.

Sana: Is it cancer?

Me: I'm sending a screenshot of my DNA relatives. Hold on.

Sana: Holy. Fuck.

Me: I know.

Sana: That can't be real. No. Are you kidding?

Me: I almost wish I was. But it makes sense, right?

Oh my god.

The other day she said something about not wanting me to repeat her mistakes.

What if she didn't mean her. But, like, a BIRTH mom?

Sana: Did you ask your parents about it?

Me: I can't. Remember when Bea decided to switch majors?

Dad shut down and stopped talking to people.

Mom started doing CrossFit.

And that wasn't nearly as big as this.

I can't breathe right now.

My heart is going to fall out of my chest.

Sana: Okay, stop. I'm coming over.

Me: No.

I can't be here.

I'll come to you.

I can't tell if I need
to wipe snow from
my frosty windshield
or tears from my eyes.

There's no way to tell except
blinking and wiping.
It's not going away.
That thing that makes it
so I can't see straight.

The snow.
The tears.
The pain.

My best friend lives in a double-wide trailer.
My parents talk about her mom
in that bad way people do when they
don't understand something.

Sana yells when she's mad.
Swear words are part of her,
like breathing.
And she pushes buttons
and parties
and smokes weed sometimes.

She doesn't follow any rules
except her own.

We shouldn't work.

But Sana champions everything
I do.

She listens to my poems before
I let anyone else see them.
She leans over my notebook
and whispers,
"It's so good."

That trailer she lives in
sometimes feels
more like home
than my own.
And her mom,
who my parents don't understand,
works two jobs
and makes me feel like I belong.

Sana is my friend.
My defender.
My person.

When Sana tells me,
"It'll be okay.
It's not okay right now,
but it will be."
I want to believe her.

But this morning
Jack did not exist to me.
And now he's taken up space in my heart
so gargantuan I think
there might not be room left for me
anymore.

He's going to grow so big,
my chest will split open,
and my guts and soul
will spill out right in front of Sana.
Then I bet she won't tell me,
"It's okay."

Sana turns on my favorite songs,
and we use her neighbor's Wi-Fi
to internet stalk the stranger I share half my DNA with.

But he's even a stranger to the internet,
a single matched result,
with a private Facebook.
His profile picture is my only clue
to who he is.

A man with a guitar cradled in his lap.
Shaggy auburn hair, eyes closed,
and a tattoo of a woman
with devil horns
on his collarbone.

Somewhere there is a world
where I grew up sitting on his lap,
tracing my fingers along
the strings of that guitar,
and finding myself in
the father I don't know.

Giggling because the mother
I don't know
is making a funny face so I'll

smile
for the picture she's taking.

Maybe she's got dark curls like me.
And writes poems
getting lost in thoughts
imagining people
she'll never know
and places
she'll never go.

To: Bea Koenig (b.koenig@brown.edu)
From: Cordelia Koenig (CordeliaBedelia99@gmail.com)
Subject: I miss my sister.

Hey,

I know I haven't emailed in a while, but I miss you. How's school?

I've been working on my senior project. Got my Gene-Quest results back today, actually.

Feeling a little down. A little misplaced. Any chance we can get a Skype date in soon?

Love,

Cordelia

When I was little, I wondered
what made me different from my family.

I couldn't understand
why none of them
needed to say something
a million times
in their heart
before they spoke
it with their tongue.

Why Mom and Bea never seem to cry
at movies I feel in my soul.
Or why Bea and Iris have the same
sense of humor. Their jokes
a connective tissue
and I'm the one struggling
to think of anything to add.
And why is Dad gentler with me
than my sisters?

Why I've always felt lonely
sitting with them at the dinner table.
Like maybe this wasn't ever supposed to be my life.
I know they feel it too.

The way they look behind my back at each other
when I say something that is too much.
Or feel things harder than they do.
Maybe it's that they don't understand me,
but it might also be because they know.

Deep down, they know.
They know
Beatrice
and
Iris
belong.

While I'm
the outlier
the piece that doesn't fit.
the one who shares nothing
but name.

The child
stuck in the middle
of a family
who would have
been just as complete
without her.

I've known.
I've been waiting for
the other shoe
to drop.
Now that it has,
I want to glue
my shoes
to my feet.

Turns out dinner isn't always the same.
When you know a secret,
everything feels like a gesture
a nod
a clue.

Iris is in trouble, see
it doesn't happen very often.
But when it does it's
hashtag unfair
and Mom and Dad are
hashtag overreacting.

Dad says,
"No legacy is so rich as honesty,"
and I laugh, not because he's funny
but because no one
knows
I know the legacy of truth
is a lie.

I am a lie.

So I say,
"Ignorance is the curse of God;
knowledge is the wing

wherewith we fly to heaven."
And he's proud, slapping his leg
and laughing.

"Exactly!" he shouts,
and points at Iris.
"Take lessons from Cordelia."

At the very end of the table
Mom cradles her lifeline wine.

Her smile is empty, studying me
like she also wants to know
which parts of me come
from other people.

To: Cordelia Koenig (CordeliaBedelia99@gmail.com)
From: Bea Koenig (b.koenig@brown.edu)
Subject: Re: I miss my sister.

School is fine. I'm hoping to finish this semester with all As and maybe stay on for summer so I can finish up school on time. Switching majors is a pain—try not to do that. Who knew that a degree in Women's Studies is about as valuable as a degree in English (no offense!)?

I'm glad you're working on your project. But I'm confused about the ancestry part. Mom said you were doing something with poetry. Do you need me to send you my GeneQuest results?

Also, what has you feeling "misplaced," or is this just a typical overly-dramatic-Cordelia moment? Honestly, babe, you've got to stop being so sensitive or you're never going to survive college.

Trust me, things will be different when you get to Columbia. You won't care about the little things you worry about now. Maybe a Skype date next week? Soooooo busy.

Love always,

Bea

Kodiak tells me about his project
like a little sea otter.
Bobbing his head up and down,
breaking it apart like it's an urchin
full of juicy meat,
tender and fulfilling.

"A modern retelling of Tlingit stories."
He's so excited
I almost forget last year happened.

I tell him how mine feels like seaweed,
tangling my toes
and keeping me down.

When he asks, "How can I help?"
I try not to let the pinprick of tears
stain the first time we've talked
really talked
in years.

"Don't cry."
His hand rises between us,
palm upturned.
He's an eagle again.
Open.

Secrets.

They are as intimate as going palm to palm.

My hand slips into his,

and it's calloused and soft at the same time.

Fingers intertwined,

his eyes staring into mine like they might swallow

what is left of me.

"I'm here if you need to talk."

At night,
when Iris texts her friends from her room
and Dad lies slumped over in an armchair
while Mom sleeps in their bed,

I study our family photos.

I look for the wave in my brown hair
and the same nose my sisters have.
I look through old photo albums in the library.
Thumbing through pictures,
vacations to Disneyland,
day trips to Seward,
nights in Alyeska
where we picked blueberries
and ate them until our fingers
were stained purple.

I find a picture of my mother,
belly fat and full of baby.
She's smiling at the camera
but her eyes are sad.
Bea hangs from her leg
with pigtails and a T-shirt that says,
I'm 3!

3.

The same age she was when I was born.

There's lurch in my stomach,

a pit

staining my heart instead of my fingers.

The question bigger now.

How?

What if I'm not adopted?

What if the answer to the question

makes it worse?

Makes the puzzle

unsolvable.

Unimaginable.

What if I'm the history

she doesn't want me to repeat?

Best Mama

Me: Mom, can I ask you a question?

Mom: Sure.

Me: Maybe I'm not adopted.

But would you tell me if I was, like, from a sperm donor

or something?

Mom: Cordelia, I don't have time for this.

I have 3 showings this afternoon.

You're not adopted.

I didn't use a sperm donor.

Do your homework.

We can talk later.

Kodiak Jones

Me: Can I ask you something hard?

Kodiak: Yeah.

Me: Last year.

When everything happened with Liv.

Did you ever feel like it was too much?

Like you were going crazy?

Kodiak: We're all a little bit crazy.

The eclectic, artist types.

But yeah. It wasn't exactly the best time in my life.

Does this have anything to do with why you were crying

the other day?

What's going on?

Me: I think my parents are lying to me about something.

Something huge.

And it's too much.

I can't believe that they'd lie to me about this.

Kodiak: Cordelia.

I hate to break it to you.

But people lie all the time.

Even parents.

Trust me. I almost was one.

Everyone knows
what happened last year.

Because Liv cried mascara streaks
at school and screamed
his name
like his soul was
being expelled
from her body.

KODIAK!

And he turned,
his face red
eyes glossy
fingers tight
into fists
while Liv spoke.

"I'm sorry.
I just couldn't."

In the crowded hallway,
everyone waited
for his reaction,
and Kodiak howled

as if his soul
was being expelled
from his body
too.

"I know,"
he sobbed,
choking on his words.
And when she reached for him
he fell apart in her arms
and he seemed little
and littler still next to her.

And everyone knows what happened after that.

Kodiak got drunk in 3rd period
and took his mom's new car
for a joyride.

He crashed,
destroying a sign,
a mailbox,
and the car
before coming back
for 5th period.

Kodiak got handcuffed
outside the school
while everyone watched.

Even Liv
who cried
and whispered,
"We'll never be the same."

People
lie all the time.

They lie about things
that bring them fear
and threaten to take
away what is
comfortable.

But blood doesn't need to lie.
DNA doesn't care if it
hurts or makes you question
your identity.

DNA makes you who
you are.
People make you question who
you are.

Sana-Friend ♥

Me: Hey.

Hypothetical question.

Sana: I love hypothetical questions!

Yes!

Wait. No!

Does this involve Emma and her being totally gay for
me?

Me: No.

Sana: Is it a writer thing or a Cordelia thing?

Me: A writer thing, for sure.

What if you knew someone was lying about a potentially
HUGE secret?

Like, life-changing huge.

And the only way to find an answer was to reach out to a
stranger?

Would you do it?

Sana: Is this about your GeneQuest results?

Me: No! I told you. It's a completely hypothetical writer
thing.

Sana: Then hypothetically

I think you should totally email your father of 99.9%
accuracy and ask him what's up.

First draft of message to Jack Bisset:

Dear Jack,

I think I might be your daughter. Or at least that's what GeneQuest says (and is apparently very accurate). This might be a little awkward, but I have a lot of questions. My parents are wonderful, but I worry they are keeping a big secret from me (i.e., you).

So what's the deal? Am I adopted? Or are you a sperm donor?

Second draft of message to Jack Bisset:

Dear Mr. Bisset,

I know this might come as a shock to you, but I think you are my father.

Trust me, it was a surprise to me too, finding your name listed as my biological father on GeneQuest, especially considering my parents, the ones who raised me the last eighteen years, have never let on that I might be adopted.

Which feels weird to say in an email.

I guess I'm going to delete this and try again sometime.

How is this so hard?

Sometimes
you don't know the question
until you're in the middle of
asking.

Sometimes
you cover the scab
you want to pick at
because you know
it might never stop
bleeding.

Sometimes
like a sled dog
carrying a team's worth
of weight
on his own,
It is too much to hold.

Sometimes
you need to unload the sled,
pick the scab,
and ask the question.

Sana and I share earbuds,
listening to her favorite songs
instead of the way our boots
crunch snow that will melt
by tomorrow.

"If we walk,
if we listen,
we might feel
better."

She always says "we"
as if our feelings are the same.
Connected like sister snowflakes
stuck to my gloves.
Most of the time I believe her,
but today her words feel all wrong.

I tell her, "Maybe I don't want to do this
anymore. This project, it's too much.
If Bea can switch her major,
I can switch my project."

"You can't go back."
She isn't wrong.

I think of my chest opening again,
bright red blood splattered across
stark white blankets of snow.

Soon it will be gone.
It's called breakup,
when the snow disappears
and the dog crap thaws
and mud and gravel
are revealed.

This is breakup for me too.
From the memory of things being the way
they were before I knew.

Clear
and close
and now gone.

GeneQuest
Genetic Family Conversations

To: Jack Bisset (last online 4 months ago)
From: Cordelia Koenig (online)

Dear Jack,

Hi. I'm reaching out because GeneQuest lists you as my father. So, I guess it's nice to meet you (sort of).

Sincerely,

Cordelia

I can't stop
looking at his face.

Waiting, as if at any moment
his Facebook profile will change
and reveal
a part of him
I couldn't see before.
I refresh my email
over.
And over.
And over.

Every time my phone
rings
or dings
or beeps
or buzzes.
I imagine he's
there
on the other end
with a reply.

I can't stop wishing the future looked
more like my past.

Hidden.
Away from sight.
Vague.

If only I could take my heart
from my chest and pot it
like a plant.
Feed it full of all the things it needs
and put it back in its home
once the hard part is over.

If I were a plant,
I wouldn't be Jack's.

He may have provided the seed,
but he didn't dig the earth
or water soil or wait through
a cold spring for my petals to
form and grow.

But I'm wilting now,
and I can't help but wonder if Jack is the
rain or the sun.
The pesticide or the fertilizer.

GeneQuest says we share
fifty percent
of what makes us
us.

Fifty percent of me
is a stranger.
And the other fifty percent
is a liar.

GeneQuest
Genetic Family Conversations

To: Cordelia Koenig *(online)*
From: Jack Bisset *(last online one hour ago)*

Wow.

I never thought I'd hear from you.

I guess you're probably wondering what happened with me and your mom? How is she, by the way? Did she ever make it as a big-time real estate agent?

Confirmation.
My.
Mom.
Had.
An.
Affair.
Which.
Means.
One.
Thing.

My dad, with his jokes
and his Shakespeare
and his classes,

is not my father.

But my mom knows Jack,
My biological father.
Enough.

The realization and the pain
it will cause my dad
and my sisters

hurts
more
than
before.

Kodiak Jones

Kodiak: Hey.

I'm running late.

Me: For what?

Kodiak: Weren't we supposed to meet up and workshop

our pieces?

Me: Crap.

I forgot.

Kodiak: That's cool. Do you want to reschedule?

Me: No.

Come over.

I could use the distraction.

Kodiak: Oh?

Me: That lie I thought my parents were telling?

Turns out I was right.

To: Cordelia Koenig (koenig.cordelia@tchs.edu)
From: Vidya Nadeer (nadeer.vidya@tchs.edu)
Subject: Re: Re: Re: Senior Project Application

Cordelia,

I've loved the recent poems you are turning in for class! I only wish you'd share them with your peers. You've grown so much in your writing this last year, and I must say I'm proud. Have you thought any more about the poetry conference? There's a contest on the last day. You'd have to recite your poem, but I really think you have a chance at winning if you put forth some effort.

Think about it.

Vidya Nadeer

To: Vidya Nadeer (nadeer.vidya@tchs.edu)
From: Cordelia Koenig (koenig.cordelia@tchs.edu)
Subject: Re: Re: Re: Re: Senior Project Application

Dear Ms. Nadeer,

Thank you so much for thinking of me in regard to the conference. I'll be sure to consider it.

Thanks again,

Cordelia Koenig

Kodiak isn't playing a part.
He's really the kind of guy who
looks like he was born with stubble
and a hoodie attached to his body.
As if his face is simultaneously pictured in the dictionary
under "cool" and "carefree."

When he parks his bike against my house
I'm already closing the front door,
pulling my beanie over my ears.
He reaches,
pulling me into a hug that
feels so familiar
I could swear I still have braces
and he's still wearing Vans.

Maybe
in another world
where Jack raised me instead of Dad,
I would have fit
with the boy
who sings his poems.

Instead,
I tug Kodiak back to my world.
Where there's a lake behind my house

and it's so cold we might freeze,
but the ice isn't thick enough to walk on.

We sit at the water's edge,
next to each other
on the dock where I learned to fish
and where my sisters and I
took turns
pushing each other in
every summer.

We're shivering but anything
is better than sitting under the roof
where the lies began.

When Kodiak stuffs his hands
into his pockets
and stares out onto the lake
I forget he's an eagle or an otter.
He's just a boy who used to
know me.

A boy who might want to know me
again.

I say, "It's so much easier to write a poem

and keep it in my notebook
than it is to say how I feel."

"But if you say it out loud,
it takes the scariness of those feelings
away."
Then he's quiet,
and the world is
crackling ice
and the still of what
used to be winter
and is now something else.

When I'm done reading my poems
he looks faraway,
and doesn't say
a word.

Doesn't try to fill up
the silence that sits between
us like another person.

But he's right.
I am free.
So I tell him about the message from
Jack.

The big secret.
I know in my heart
what Jack meant when he asked
about Mama.

They have a history:
Me.

Kodiak's breath puffs out in tiny clouds,
and he takes his hands out of his pockets
and reaches for mine.

Pulling me to a stand,
he tucks my hair back
into my beanie and holds me there a moment.
"It's okay to be sad, Cordelia.
This is sad."

Sana-Friend ♥

Sana: In case you were wondering . . .

My neighbor was not joking about paying me in cigarettes.

Me: That's disgusting.

When are you going to tell her you don't smoke?

Sana: Absolutely NEVER!

God Cordelia. Think about my street cred.

Me: What was I thinking?

Sana: I ask myself that constantly.

WHAT is Cordelia thinking?

Me: Hey I'm headed to bed.

I'll see you at school tomorrow.

Sana: Dude you're being weird. It's like 8.

Me: I know.

Sana: You know you're being weird or you know it's 8?

Me: Both.

Sana: Are you okay?

Me: I don't know.

Sana: Do you want me to come over?

Hey.

Cordelia?

CORDELIA ANN KOENIG!

Sister Bea

Bea: I sent you my GeneQuest results.

Me: I don't need them.

Bea: Mom said you've been having a hard time.

And I went back and checked. I never sent them!

She's worried.

But having a hard enough time you can't do your own

project?

Come on Delia. That's not like you.

Me: Yeah.

Bea: You should talk to Mom.

Me: I can't.

Bea: Why?

Me: I can't.

Bea: Want to know what I think?

I think you're just going through some sort of senior year

crisis of self.

I went through the same thing, which is why I did the

ancestry project.

Because I wanted to learn who I was.

Where I came from.

And know what I found out?

Our family is really cool.

We're related to Emmeline Pankhurst!

Me: Trust me. It's not a crisis of self.

Bea: But knowing I was related to her.

She's like the best feminist.

It's half the reason I chose Brown for Women's Studies.

I promise. It'll get better next year when you're at college.

Me: This is different.

Bea: Yeah, I know.

It's always different with you.

Like in third grade when you asked to go by Hannah instead of Cordelia.

Or a few years ago when you decided you were vegan.

How long did that last again? Five minutes? Ten?

Know what I think?

Me: What?

Bea: I think you were hoping your results would be different.

That you were switched at birth or something.

And now you're disappointed.

Me: I promise you, it's not like that.

Bea: You aren't that special.

We are all individuals trying to get our needs met.

And you're alienating the people who love you.

Iris said you've been acting really weird too.

And Mom said you've been hanging out with Kodiak again.

She's worried.

Me: I bet she is.

I'd be worried if I was Mom too.

Bea: What is that supposed to mean?

Me: Nothing.

Forget it.

To: Cordelia Koenig (CordeliaBedelia99@gmail.com)
From: Bea Koenig (b.koenig@brown.edu)
Subject: Your Project

Here.

42% German/French

31.5% British/Irish

22% Scandinavian

2.6% Broadly Southern European

1.25% Broadly European

0.3% North African and Arabian

0.2% Native American

Truth is,
we aren't so different
anyway.

Just numbers
and words
on a page.

As quickly as winter came
sneaking in
with a slow morning frost,
then all at once,
snow—

I wake up, and it's gone,
vanished.

Mom doesn't understand
I don't care about her chores.
I can't wash away the email
in my in-box
that spells out a story
she doesn't want me to hear.
I can't wash away
the remnants of last night's
salmon eggs benedict
Dad made for dinner
while listening to NPR podcasts.

I can't wash away the guilt
of imagining a world
where the man who raised me
didn't exist.

Where the man who didn't
was my world,
and instead of plays
he gave me concerts.

Dad doesn't know
that within the walls of my in-box
is an email
from a man
he's never heard of.
A man who is
also
my father.

Why should I care about dishes
when winter is gone
and so is my ignorance?
To go back to days
when the snow kept away
the dirt and gravel beneath.

I want winter back.

Sana-Friend ♥

Sana: I know things are weird for you right now.

But what are you doing this weekend?

Me: Wallowing.

Trying to decide how to ask my mom if I'm the product

of an affair.

Sana: Wait. Wut?

I thought you were adopted?

Me: Me too.

It's complicated.

Sana: Oh Delia.

I don't know what to say.

Me: Me either.

So what are you doing this weekend?

Did you want to work on the written portion of your

project?

Sana: Hell no!

So I feel kind of weird saying this now.

Me: What?

Sana: I heard back from UAA.

Which is in Anchorage, I know, but at least I have that

safety net.

I'm officially going to college!

Me: Why would you feel weird saying that?!

That's awesome!

Sana: I know!

Interested in a distraction to get your mind off that dumpster fire?

Me: Yes. Dumpster fire is a perfect way to describe what has become my life.

Sana: I'm going to a party to celebrate my being a college student and all.

Fletcher Wilson is having a bonfire.

It's gonna be liiiiiit.

Me: . . .

Sana: A girl can try.

So how're you going to ask your mom about all this?

Me: No idea. I tried to talk to Bea about it.

Kinda.

Sana: I can only imagine how well that went over with Queen Bea.

What did you say?

Me: I didn't get to say much before she was telling me . . .

What was it?

I'm "just going through a senior year crisis of self."

Sana: Sounds like her.

Me: And as soon as she said, "We are all individuals trying to get our needs met," I stopped talking to her.

Sana: College does not look good on her.

Me: Life doesn't look good on her.

Sana: Yeah.

She's always had a sour vibe.

I say you rip off the band-aid.

Sit your mom down.

Hold her hand.

Say "I've got something to tell you."

Me: "Hey, I know you boned a guy named Jack Bisset roughly eighteen years ago."

Sana: I think that sums it up.

Me: Why is thinking about these conversations so much easier than actually having them? Crap.

I gotta go.

Dinner.

It's the way Dad lingers behind Mom.
Playful, she's making herself a plate
while he's dancing a finger along her side.
And she giggles
in that way girls do
when they flirt with boys.

I wonder if Mom flirted with Dad
back when she slept with Jack.
Or if she couldn't sleep at night because
she was scared of getting caught.

Did she cry when the snow went away
because she knew there was nothing
to cover the earth anymore?

Or did she smile at Dad
and touch his arm
and kiss him more
so he wouldn't wonder?

If I try hard enough,
and hold my breath,
maybe I can forget I'm
at dinner with my family.

Maybe I can go outside.
Away from here,
and them.
Stare long enough at the sky
and beg the clouds to form
baby snowflakes
so maybe winter
can last
a little
bit
longer.

Mom knocks on my door
the way she did when I was little.
"Hey, the dishes . . ."

I tell her I don't want to do them
and she stares.
Silent.
Like she's waiting for me to
laugh,
say I'm kidding,
or apologize
because I didn't vacuum either.

I don't.
Because I'm tired of holding
her secret.

I want to be free
like an eagle
and spread
my arms
when I share my poems.

"Well, remember to pick up Iris
after school tomorrow,"
before she eases the door closed.

I wanted her to fight.
To say, "Young lady, ·
what has gotten into you?"

Then I could tell her everything.
Show her the emails.
Scream.

But she doesn't.
And I'm afraid
it's because she also knows
or at least suspects
our winter is over.

Kodiak Jones

Me: Another hard question.

Kodiak: Go for it.

Me: Last year,

after everything.

Did you ever wish you could go back in time?

Erase.

Start over?

Kodiak: Probably not.

At the very least

I learned from my mistakes.

Me: No part of you wonders what could have been done

differently?

Are you serious?

Kodiak: I've had a lot of time to think about it.

Like even when we were "happy" and in love,

We weren't right for each other.

Liv was too wild,

and I had a hard time keeping up.

And by the time everything went down—

it was like I felt I had to make it work.

We were having a kid together.

We had a plan and everything.

Me: I can't even imagine.

Kodiak: Yep. We were picking out names.

Talking about how we were going to tell our parents.

Even looking into getting an apartment.

Me: That sounds terrifying.

Kodiak: Don't get me wrong. What happened felt awful.

I never want to relive that pain.

But at least I'm not where I was a year ago.

Does that make sense?

Me: Not the way I think I want it to.

Kodiak: Backward is never forward. Going back is just going back to a bad thing.

And now things are okay.

I'm all lined up for UAA in the fall.

Maybe going away for school after I get my GPA up.

It's a whole different future now.

What's going on?

What do you want to erase?

Me: Everything.

GeneQuest
Genetic Family Conversations

To: Cordelia Koenig *(online)*
From: Jack Bisset *(online)*

Hey.

I haven't heard back from you, and I realize how vague my last email sounded.

I'm hoping for a chance to explain myself. First, I want you to know that I loved your mother. Really loved her. Even though I knew she was married and knew what we were doing was wrong, I thought she was the most beautiful woman I'd ever met. It's the kind of love that crept out of nowhere and left me blind when she told me we couldn't see each other anymore. I thought that someday she was going to leave her husband and we were going to be together. It's probably an awful thing to say, considering I'm guessing that's the guy who raised you. Maybe I'm bitter. I found out about you the week before I left Tundra Cove for Seattle, and it damn near killed me knowing I'd never meet you.

She came over, told me she was pregnant, and made it clear that she didn't want me involved.

I didn't want that.

I wanted a chance to be your dad.

For what it's worth, I'm sorry. I hope you've had a good life. I hope your parents are happy and everything. I just wanted a chance to tell you my side of things.

Jack

I can't do this.

His unfiltered words
spread through my chest,
making it hot
like asphalt in summer
too hot to touch.
Knowing too much,
the little details.
Where he lives,
what he wanted,
and that he
loved
my mother.

That he knew about me.

He wanted me,
and ached the same way
I ache.
Wondering for years
which parts of me
were living out there
looking like him.
Wishing we'd gotten a chance
at a life together.

Did he dance fingers
up Mom's side
at dinner?
And did he cry when
she told him
he couldn't keep me
the way Kodiak did
when Liv told him
they couldn't
keep their baby?

There is no going back after this.
There's no way I can't read this over
and over
and over
Forever.

Because I know at last
I'm not only a lie
but a product of
infidelity.
A sin.
A sob story.
A secret.

I am the thing people
whisper about.

So I make a choice.

Sana-Friend ♥

Sana: Are you out of class yet?

Me: Need a ride home?

Sana: I HEARD BACK FROM UNIVERSITY OF DENVER!

Me: I take it that your all caps indicated this was a positive experience?

Sana: FUCK YES it was!

I mean

There's no possible way I can afford to go without a scholarship.

Like. Zero way.

But I like knowing that I at least got in.

Me: That's amazing!

Let's go celebrate!

Sana: Later?

I'm going to Maddy's house to work on our projects.

Me: Oh cool.

Sana: You could probably come over too.

But I did see YOUR partner hanging out in the commons area.

Playing guitar.

Brooding and such.

Kodiak's fingers press
down on guitar strings
with the same familiarity
he recites his poems.
Only this time,
when he sings
out into the commons,
the lyrics to the plucky
acoustic sound
of his guitar.

He sings his poems,
then mine.

Eyes closed,
chest open,
and my stomach
tumbles
each time
he sings
one of my
lines.

I can't help
how I want to reach out
and brush my fingers

against his eyelashes.
I want to hide in the safe place
between his shoulder
and chest,
and never come back
to the hurting place
I'm in now.

To dot with my lips
every freckle
spread across his nose.

"The songs are beautiful,"
I say.

"Of course they are."
He opens his eyes
and whispers to me,
our knees touching,
"You wrote them."

Missed call from Mom- 3:32 pm

Missed call from Mom- 3:33 pm

Text from Mom- What are you doing?

Where are you?

Missed call from Dad- 3:40 pm

Text from Sana- You need to get a room.

But srsly you guys are totally cute.

Missed call from Mom- 3:44 pm

Text from Dad- Honey, are you okay?

Missed call from Mom- 3:45 pm

Missed call from Mom- 3:46 pm

Text from Mom- Cordelia. You'd better have a damn good
reason for not picking up your sister.

His fingers
on mine.
We clutch the guitar together
"This is G."
He slides my finger to the left
"And E. Like this."

His breath
against my neck
makes my whole body
tingle.
Nervous
because we are so close
all I need
is to turn
ever so slightly
and our lips
might meet
and our hearts
might explode.

I start to turn,
and my cheek
brushes his.
His finger
tilts my chin

toward him
and we are about
to kiss
when his phone rings.

"It's your mom.
I think she's upset."

Red.
Hot.
Anger.
Mom's scream rang through the phone.
"I can't believe you forgot her!
What were you doing?
Of course you were with him."

I can't say anything
because my words are lost
as if they've drifted
a thousand miles out
from my mind's shore.

I want to be sorry,
but I'm not,
because my mom lied
the ultimate lie.
My heart hurts,
aching more today
than yesterday.
And the only thing that
has made me feel good
since I found out
is the feeling

of Kodiak's
cheek
against mine.

Sana-Friend ♥

Sana: Dude.

Your mom called my phone.

Like a lot.

Me: I figured.

Sana: WTF happened?

Her voicemail sounded PISSED.

Me: I forgot Iris at practice.

Sana: Oh shit.

No wonder she's pissed.

And you were with Kodiak

Me: We were doing senior project stuff.

Sana: Is that code for wiener and vagine stuff?

I saw you guys.

Damn girl.

This isn't just a crush anymore is it?

Me: I don't know.

Sana: Be careful.

You're gonna end up pregnant like Liv.

Have to transfer to a school in Anchorage.

That's a long drive Cordelia.

Me: Well, that was called for.

Sana: . . .

Wow.

Okay.

Sorry.

I didn't realize it was such a sensitive subject for you.

Me: It's a fucking sensitive subject for everyone.

She had an abortion, Sana.

Sana: Whoa.

Yeah.

I get that it's a big fucking deal.

But it's us.

Me: I know. Sorry.

It's just been a long day.

And my mom is pissed.

And Iris was so mad she wouldn't look at me the whole

way home.

Just stared out the window.

Sana: Uh. Yeah.

That sucks.

It'll blow over though. Right?

Me: Gotta go.

Mom's coming.

"What were you thinking?"
Mom hisses.

"I don't know."
I don't know anything anymore.

"You left her all alone."
I know.
"What if something happened?
And what are you thinking,
being around
that boy?"

I tell Mom that boy isn't all bad.
She should know,
it's her friend's son,
after all.
We've spent time together.
She watched him grow up,
from a boy
into *that* boy.

Mom clutches my doorknob,
pulling it behind her
and leaning down,

quiet at first
like the threat of her voice
is so heavy
it can't be anything
but whispered.

"Boys like that
will eat you up
and spit you out
before you ever
know what happened.

"Boys like that will
hurt you in ways
you never knew you
could hurt.

"Boys like Kodiak
have a history,
you know.

He's like . . ."

"Who, Mom?"

"Nothing. Never mind."

"Who?!"

"He's like . . ."

His name
feels like Voldemort
on my tongue.

He who must not be
named.

He who must not be
remembered
or acknowledged
or even discussed.

He.
The evil thing
that must be expelled from our lives.
Banished.
Trashed.
And I'm just the girl
who lives
because of it.

I let his name rest on my tongue,
stretching my teeth
around those four little letters
I've been holding inside
for days.

"He's like Jack?"

Mom takes too long
before the realization hits her face.

Like it had to travel
from her ears
to her brain
and then
finally
her
mouth.

She starts to talk
a dozen times.
Parting her lips
to choke on
words she probably never
dreamed
she'd have to say.
"Did you just—"
She can't even repeat
his name.

I want to feel
bigger
stronger somehow

for breaking her apart
the way I feel broken.
Shattered,
and splintered
like fallen icicles on pavement.
But I just feel little
and littler still
next to her.

"How?"
Mom asks,
a single word
caught
at the edge
of a whisper.

"GeneQuest."

She crumbles.
And part of me,
just part,
feels bad.

"You have to understand
things were different.
Your dad and me—
We were going through
a rough time—"

"Which one?"

"Oh my god.
Cordelia.
I mean your *father*.

Jack—he was a mistake,
my beautiful girl."

All emotion welling
like fish swimming
beneath the surface
of ice.
I can see just
enough
to know its danger.

"If he was a mistake,
then I was a mistake."

When you looked into my eyes
and told me I wasn't his.
I cried.

Not because you took away the only
father
I've ever known.

But because I was relieved.

I always knew there was something different about me.

When you looked into my eyes
and told me not to tell him
I cried.

Not because you wanted me to lie.

But because you deepened the gap between me
and the only
father
I've ever known.

It will never be okay.

I will never be able to hug my dad without a voice in my
ear
as loud as the Russian River during peak salmon season,
screaming wild rapids, hissing.
He's not really yours.
This isn't real.
You are living a lie.

Heart.

Explosion.

Like the Fourth of July
when it's midnight
and still light outside.

I can see everything
without the mystery of darkness.

What should be magical
is only daytime
and the vague outline
of what might be fireworks.

I'd give anything
for my magic back.
To hear my father,
my Shakespeare-loving
father,
tell me she's wrong.

Heart.

Implosion.

"The thing about Jack,
he's not a good guy.
He's not a dad
kind of guy."

"How could you?"
I'm hissing,
like a lynx protecting
its baby.
Only my mama is the thing
that threatens.

"Were you ever
going to tell me?"

"I don't know.
It doesn't change anything,
does it?
Your dad is still your dad.
This guy is just
a guy.
Honey.

Please."

"It.
Changes.
Everything."

When Dad knocks,
we both jump.

He does that thing
he always does.
Happy, cutting through
our tension when he asks,
"What are my girls squabbling about?"
He ruffles my hair,
nuzzles Mom,
and when she
looks into my eyes
she's pleading.

Please.
Don't tell him.

Mom looks like she's
about to lose it.
Her skin, red and veiny

like skinned moose meat
left open
to rot.

She brings a fingernail
up to her mouth,
chewing on the corner.
Even her eyelashes
quiver.

Kodiak Jones

Kodiak: Pretty crazy day

Me: You have no idea.

Kodiak: Is it just me

or did it almost go too far?

It's probably a good thing your mom called.

Me: What?

Kodiak: Come on.

You know we couldn't come back from something like

that.

Me: Oh.

Yeah. No, I agree.

Kodiak: Did you get in a lot of trouble?

Me: Probably not as much as I should have been.

I asked her about Jack.

Sort of a distraction.

Kodiak: Holy shit!

Delia!

Are you okay?

What did she say?

Me: Ohhhh.

Nothing crazy.

Just that I was right.

And my dad doesn't know.

So yeah.

Pretty crazy day.

Kodiak: Shit.

My friends just showed up.

I'll call you in a while.

Sana-Friend ♥

Me: What are you doing tonight?

Sana: That party at Fletcher's I told you about.

I'm gonna go find out exactly what Emma Daniels means by "It's complicated" on her Facebook.

Me: You still use Facebook?

Sana: Nope.

But it is part of my 32-step internet sleuthing process.

Me: Take me with you.

Sana: To internet sleuth?

Dude.

I do it right here on my computer.

It's a dark dirty path though.

I don't know if you're up for it.

Me: No.

To Fletcher's.

Sana: Are you kidding me right now?

No. You're joking.

Don't be a tease.

That's messed up.

All you straight girls.

Me: I had a bad day.

Pick me up at nine?

Sana: No way I'm going out before ten.

Won't your parents care?

Me: Not tonight they won't.

Jack Bisset has an Instagram.
I find it when I search for his name
plus "Seattle."

Two thousand
two hundred
eighty
miles
away.

His pictures show a life
like a rock star's.
There's one of him
with a cigarette in his mouth
where smoke conceals most
of his features like fog
above the mountains
outside my home.

Girls hanging on his arm
in one photo.
Another has him on a
motorcycle
probably driving away from
the history
I live in.

Then the one I saw before
on his Facebook.
Him playing guitar
and with a tattoo
of a woman
on his chest.
She's got devil horns.

I'm seeing it now,
her long brown hair,
hazel eyes,
and a smirk,
like she's got nothing to lose.
And I guess she doesn't.

A striking resemblance
to the woman a room over
who shares the other half
of my DNA.

GeneQuest
Genetic Family Conversations

To: Jack Bisset *(last online 2 minutes ago)*
From: Cordelia Koenig *(online)*

Hi Jack,

Sorry it took so long to message you back.

As you can imagine, this week has been a little crazy, and I'm still trying to unpack everything. It's weird to think that a week ago, I didn't know about you.

And now here you are.

So, for the sake of getting to know each other, what's it like to live in Seattle? I've only ever been once when I was really little.

GeneQuest
Genetic Family Conversations

To: Cordelia Koenig *(online)*
From: Jack Bisset *(online)*

Wow. I didn't realize you just found out. I assumed you knew, and that's why you took the GeneQuest test.

That's got to be hard, kid. I'm sorry. I've wondered about you every day since, but I didn't know what to do. I took the test hoping you might look me up one day. I hoped we'd get in touch and be able to talk, but I didn't want it to be like this—a total surprise for you. I can't imagine. It's crazy that it's happened now. You must have been pretty upset. I can't believe your parents didn't tell you.

Seattle is amazing. I've been here 18 years now. I guess it's home. The city has become my playground. I am a music producer, so it's a perfect place for that. Lots of young musicians and incredible bands. How are things back in Alaska?

How is your mom? Does she know we have been talking?

GeneQuest
Genetic Family Conversations

To: Jack Bisset *(online)*
From: Cordelia Koenig *(online)*

Hello Jack,

A music producer? I don't think I've ever met (much less been
related to) someone that cool. Have you worked with anyone
I might know about? Mom's good. Her real-estate business
really blew up a few years ago, so she's been busy. And
she knows we talk. I asked her what happened after the big
message you sent. She's for sure cool with it.

I know this is kind of weird, but can I call you?

Cordelia

"For sure"
Mom knows.

But Dad still has no idea.
I wonder if he knew
there was even a Jack Bisset
in existence.

If asked,
would he draw a blank?
Ponder if it's a Shakespearean actor
he should know about?

While Mom knows
I found Jack,
she never asked
if I messaged him
or wanted to talk to him
or planned to talk to him.

But she's got to assume
that my curiosity
and yearning for truth
would lead to inevitable contact.

So yes,

she knows.
Or at least,
she should.

It's 7:22 pm
when I call the number
he gave me.

At first the other end
is crackling in and out
of service
and I have to say hello
three times
before I hear anything
back.

"Hi.
Yeah.
I'm here."

His voice is higher pitched than I imagined.
And I wonder if he is thinking
my voice doesn't match my pictures either.
If he even looked up my pictures.

My heart is jumping around my chest,
ping-ponging from side to side while I figure out what
to say next.

"This is weird,"
I say,
and when he doesn't respond
right away
I think I must have said the wrong thing.

But then,
"Yeah, kid.
This is weird."

We talk for an hour.
He tells me about his band.
And that his recording studio
is right downtown—
he sees the ocean every day
on his way home.

"Yeah, I work with a lot of local artists.
Ever hear of Pentalux?
They were in the studio last week."

I tell him I love poetry.
How the sound of acoustic guitar
makes my heart thrum,
and he chuckles on the other end of the phone
and it sounds melodious,
like he's wrapped in delight.
"You get that from me."

He tells me I should check out
the MTV Unplugged album with Nirvana
and that he never
got over Kurt Cobain's death.

I want to say my nirvana
is daydreaming a life

where my mom didn't lie
and I got to know him
while I was growing up.

But instead,
I keep my daydream,
writing a secretive story in my head
that I can visit
anytime
the pain gets
too real.

If I told Kodiak
I was talking to Jack
he'd do the right thing.
He'd come over
and let me sing a poem,
and when we got close enough,
he'd remind me what a bad
idea it is
for us to kiss.

If I told Sana
she'd make a joke,
and forget
that not everyone
administers comedy
for pain.

I want to tell someone
my secrets.
About the father I never knew.

Anyone.
But it's all too messed up.
I'll just keep it in,
holding fragile eggs
with barbed fingers.

Jack Bisset

> **Me:** Back then.
>
> When you had to leave.
>
> How did you get it to stop hurting?
>
> **Jack:** I didn't.
>
> It still hurts.
>
> But at least now we can know each other.
>
> **Me:** We can.

9:55 pm
As I leave
for the party
Iris is sitting in the hall
playing on her phone.
Hashtag bored.
She doesn't look up,
but I crawl next to her,
resting my chin
on her soft brown hair.

"I'm sorry
I didn't remember
to get you."

"It's okay,"
she says.
"But you're being weird.
Weirder than normal."
Tears in every corner of her eyes
like pools of raindrops,
she's waiting for me to say something.

"You've got to be nicer to Mom.
All your fighting.

She cries every day,
did you know?"

I cringe,
hold Iris's hand in mine
careful
like she's the most brittle layer of spruce bark
I'm peeling away from a tree.

She'll never know her mom,
and my mom,
are different people.
One loves,
the other lies.

If Jack was my father
maybe we'd split time
between here and Seattle.

Maybe Alaska would be our summers.
Seattle, our rainy winters.

Maybe Iris wouldn't be here,
and maybe she would.

Maybe Mom would've
dyed her hair a bright color—like green—
and quit real estate to follow Jack.
Maybe Mom wouldn't be so uptight,
and maybe Bea wouldn't be so uptight either.
Maybe Dad wouldn't tease
and run fingers up Mom's side
or look so happy all the time.

Maybe he wouldn't have his Shakespeare
or his smile for me only.
Maybe Dad wouldn't be Dad,
but a guy Mom used to know.
And this realization paralyzes my heart,
like it's been kicked out of my chest.

When Sana arrives
it's like cool pine
wafts through
our windows.

She's the breath of freshness
I needed after a day
filled with anger
and sadness.

Mom sits on the couch
tearstained eyes
with fingernails between her teeth
and doesn't say a word
about me leaving.

Dad has his arm around her,
and nuzzles her like a puppy.
He's got no idea
the reason she's crying
isn't because I'm being awful.

It's because I caught her
in the only lie
that could tear us apart.

"Where goeth thee?"
Dad bellows.

"Out," I say.

"Okay," he says,
watching me,
as I fight back the fear
he's expecting something more.
I miss him already,
this man,
missing from my "Maybe" life.

"Call me if you need a ride.
Be safe, my Cordelia.
Be true."

If he knew . . .
Maybe I wouldn't have been Cordelia.

Cordelia was the daughter who loved
her father,
King Lear,
but with all her heart.
Not for what he could give her,
not for what he could provide.
But for who he was.

He might have named me
Regan
or
Goneril,
the sisters whose love was fake.

As manufactured
as my mother's lie.

Winter may be gone
but the chill in my bones
makes it hard to breathe.

Fletcher's parents are building a cabin
ten miles out of town.
But on weekends
when the builders are gone
and his parents are at home
he throws a bonfire
in a muddy pit.

When the weather's right,
it is the place
they all go to hang out
and drink
and yell.

The fire rages,
orange and yellow and crimson,
burning as loud as
the party surrounding it.

We get to play in the dark,
hidden behind trees that keep our secrets.

Xtratufs and
fleece-lined leggings,
still in parkas
until we've all had
enough beers
to stay warm.

A party,
spring,
in Alaska.

Sana knows everyone
and when we get out of the car
she screams about her college news
then everyone screams her name back.
It still amazes me she is mine.
Her friends are my friends by proxy,
a connection
to the pulse of every party.

My people live in libraries,
not hidden away in the woods
drinking around a bonfire.
But enclosed in books,
released only by an evening
tucked away between pages.

Fletcher hands us drinks,
something fruity and pink,
and it tastes too sweet,
but I drink it anyway.

"Where's Kodiak?" he asks,
like I should know.
"He said he was coming."

When I shrug in response,
Fletcher looks confused.
"I thought you were hanging out."

I take a long swig of the pink drink
and shrug again.

It's not like that.
I wish it was,
but it's not.

This isn't my first drink.
It's not even my second.
But it is the first time
I have ever
drunk
to forget.

To forget Bea's attitude
and Iris's face after I forgot to get her.
How she asked me to be nice to Mom.
Dad's jokes I don't deserve.
Jack's confession
and my back-and-forth texts with him.
Mom's lie.
Kodiak and our almost kiss.
Our almost kiss
and our almost everything.

The drinks must be working
because for a while I do forget.
And Sana and I laugh until we cry
when we walk farther into the woods
dark skies
deep forest
and rooted path.
We're dancing,
pretending to be moon witches
and hold hands
then whisper how much we love each other.
Connected like sister snowflakes,
which feels perfect right now.

When we hear voices up ahead
it's not immediately clear
who we are hearing.

"Maybe this is just a door
that wasn't ready
to be open
until now,"
we hear a girl say.

Sana whispers close,
"Come on.

You don't want to see this."

I shake her off.
Maybe I don't want to see this
but I need to.

It's not immediately clear
that the shape of the person
beyond the thick birch trees is Liv.
That the hoodie strings she's playing with
belong to Kodiak.
I'm not certain that I hear her laughing
or see him stretch an arm out over her shoulders
pulling her into a hug
and
kissing her forehead.

"I feel really good about this,"
he says back.

It may not be immediately clear
but when it does dawn on me
what I'm seeing
I wish it wasn't.

"Hey, Delia—come here."
Sana doesn't look mad,
but a strange combination of
confused
and worried,
like she's battling between
spring and winter the way I have.
"Maybe you should cool it,"
Sana moves me closer to the bonfire.
"How many have you had?"

But I don't know.
I don't care.
I don't want to.

I love the way the pink drink
puts warm giggles in my belly.
How my cares are a memory
I won't have to deal with
until tomorrow.
And it doesn't matter who
my father is.
Or who Kodiak is
talking to.
I'm having fun tonight.

Fletcher curls an arm around me,
smiling at Sana like a halibut,
lopsided and lazy.
"Give her a break, Sana.
She's just letting loose—aren't you, Cordelia?"

"You know I've always liked you?"
Fletcher whispers in my ear,
and it's hot and wet,
and sloppy.

"Really?" I ask,
because it's the first time
anyone
has ever told me
they liked me.

"Yeah . . ."

Fletcher sits next to me on a log
And even though the bonfire
is the only warmth we need,
he wraps a blanket over our shoulders
and leans in close.
His eyes have no starlight.
They're lax around the edges,
and a little sad.

I'm sad too.

And when I look across the flicker
of fire in front of me,
I see Sana on the other side.
She smiles,
but shakes her head at the same time.
Shrugging, as if to say:
What are you gonna do?

I don't remember deciding it would happen,
but Fletcher's mouth is on mine,
and it's foggy and sluggish
like his eyes.
Our arms are somewhere,
and I can't tell if

this is something I want to do,
or just another way to forget the fact
that Kodiak is here with Liv.

When we come up for air
and I wipe the corners of my mouth,
he whispers something like,
"You're so pretty."
I look away
from his compliment
back through the fire,
flickering and hot.

Beyond the pit,
near the trees,
Liv nudges Kodiak
—looking at me with Fletcher
the way I
was looking at her with Kodiak
before.

He's already watching us,
and does that chin-tilt thing
boys do to say hi.

I don't know if it's hurt
lining the rims of his eyes
that I see,
or that I want to see.

Daddio

Me: Ccome get me?

Dad: Sure thing, honey. Everything okay?

Me: Dn't b mad.

I'm drnk.

Dad: See you soon.

Dad tells me I stink like a cotton candy distillery.
Only then do I get a sickening squeeze
in my stomach from all the sweetness
in that pink drink.

"For a quart of ale is a dish for a princess.
My princess,
are you okay?"

He's happy,
but the light in his eyes
fills me with sadness
so heavy
my head droops
against the window.

He's here
because he doesn't know
the enormous tree trunk
growing between us
has roots so deep and hidden
I don't think we'll ever really
heal.

"Honey?" he presses,
pulling the car over

to the side of a forgotten dirt road.
The night is full of stars,
but he doesn't look to them.
His eyes follow me.
"Did something happen back there?"

The lie is eating me from inside.
I tell Dad the smallest part
of the smallest truth
I can give him.
"I kissed the wrong guy."

"Now, that doesn't sound like you.
Why'd you kiss one guy
if you like another?"

"Because the one I like is trouble,
or troubled,"
I can't tell anymore.

"'The course of true love never did run smooth.'
This about Kodiak?
Tell me, Cordelia:
Why do you like him?"

The more I talk about Kodiak,
the more I think about Jack.

And before I know it,
I'm saying all the things,
I shouldn't say to Dad,
without betraying Mom's lie.
I'm sobbing, saying things like:

I can't be with him.
If I'm close with him,
it could change everything.
Dad, it could hurt you.

He holds me,
shoulders square,
forcing me to fix
my fuzzy eyes
on him.

"Cordelia."
He puts my face in his hands,
and it is warmer than I have ever remembered.

"'I love you more than words can wield the matter
Dearer than eye-sight,
space,
and liberty.
Beyond what can be valued.'
I am proud to call you my daughter.
I am proud to be your dad.
No boy can change that."

There,
in the 5-star safety-test-rated Volvo
somewhere between winter and spring
while my phone is filled
with texts
from the dad that might have been:
I think, maybe,
the fireworks
might light up the dark skies
this year.

Sana-Friend ♥

Sana: Dude.

Emma Fucking Daniels is here.

Also I talked to your boy.

Me: I told m Dad.

Sana: Wait what?

Are you kidding?

Me: Wait.

Not Jack.

Fletcher.

I'm gng to b sick.

Sana: Uhhhh.

Want me to come over?

Cordelia?

Deeeeeeeelia.

Hope you're taking a giant Advil and drinking a gallon of water.

Late in the night
my door opens
and Mom sits
at the edge of the bed
while I pretend
I'm still asleep.

She sniffles back tears.
I can hear her biting her nails
and mumbling after she works
herself into saying something.

"I know you're awake."
She whispers her words
like she doesn't know how
to use her full voice anymore.

"I can't expect you to ever understand.
how I could do something
keep something
so big from you.
That guy—
your—
he—"
Then silence.

She's crying,
in such a soft, broken way
that I want to reach out and hold her hand,
but I can't bring myself to move.
Eventually, she stands
and as she walks to the door says
one more thing
before she goes.

"Jack was never what I thought he was.
I tried for a long time to believe in his lies.
Your dad is, though. He's a good person.
If he knew it would kill him."

Things Iris says to me in the morning:
Hashtag hungover
Hashtag wasted pants
Hashtag fell asleep in the bathroom
Hashtag mom is pissed
Hashtag smells like butt
Hashtag probably grounded
Hashtag college prep

Kodiak: How's the hangover?

Me: Must you ask?

Kodiak: I didn't know you were going out last night.

Me: Me either.

I mean

I didn't know you were going out last night.

Kodiak: Such a shame.

We could have carpooled.

Then maybe I could've protected you from getting

Fletchered.

Me: Oh god.

They have a name for it? Ew!

As if I already didn't feel bad enough.

Kodiak: It's a damn shame, Cordelia.

Now that you've kissed my friend

I guess it means it'll never happen for us.

Me: Oh.

Yeah.

Kodiak: I'm joking.

That's a joke. You okay?

Me: Yeah, sorry.

Super hungover.

It's like I've gone out
to the mudflats
where the signs
warn people
to stay off.

I'm standing still
at first.
But the water starts to rise
and the silt softens around my boots.
Before I know it,
I'm stuck.

I can't breathe,
only watch
as the ocean's tide moves
closer.

I know,
like we all know,
I'm stuck
and I can't save myself
from drowning.

If only
I'd known
"We"
were an option.

Kodiak

Kodiak: Moving on.

Have you turned in pages to Ms. Nadeer lately?

Me: No.

I've been busy screwing up my life.

And unearthing family secrets.

Kodiak: And making out with Fletcher Wilson.

Me: Can we be done talking about that already?

Kodiak: Let's meet up. We can workshop some pages.

Get Ms. Nadeer something to read.

I've got community service from 1-3. That's it.

Me: I feel pretty sick.

And I've got a sneaking suspicion my parents won't
want me leaving the house after last night.

Sana-Friend ♥

Sana: Morrow dear friend.

How art thou?

Me: Please stop.

Sana: What's wrong?

Get too much of a pep talk last night from Pops?

Me: *grumble*

Sana: It's a bummer you had your dad pick you up so early.

You missed all the action.

Me: Yeah? Finally figure out if Emma Daniels is gay?

Sana: Omigherd.

Stop making everything about Emma Daniels and her sexuality. I thought you were more progressive than that.

But no. No confirmation but I will say this . . .

Between finding out about Denver and hanging out with Emma

I'm calling last night a win.

Me: So what happened?

Sana: Wait.

You don't know?

Me: Liv.

Kodiak.

All the booze.

Made out with . . .

Ugh.

Yeah, no, I don't think I would've remembered.

Even if I was there.

Sana: I might have yelled at your boy.

Me: Please.

Can we not call Fletcher that?

Sana: I'm not talking about Fletcher you dope.

I'm talking about Kodiak.

Me: SANA!

Tell me you didn't say anything stupid.

Sana: I didn't say anything stupid.

Me: Tell me you didn't say anything about me.

Sana: I can't do that.

Me: WHAT DID YOU SAY?

Sana: That he shouldn't have brought Liv to a party and flaunted that in front of you.

Then as a grand finale I asked where the hell he got off leading you on.

Me: SANA.

I can't believe you did that!

I'm so embarrassed!

You said this in front of Liv?!

Sana: I think you mean to say THANK YOU.

And no.

She left like thirty seconds after you did.

That's about the time he called Fletcher out for kissing you.

Kodiak

Me: Wait.

You got mad at Fletcher for kissing me?

Kodiak: I don't know what you're talking about.

Me: Sana told me you called him out.

Why?

Kodiak: It's nothing.

Me: But why?

Kodiak: I don't know.

I was mad at him.

Me: Why were you mad at him?

Kodiak: Please.

Can we not do this?

Me: Why were you mad at him?

Kodiak: I wasn't exactly mad at him.

I was more mad at myself.

So I took it out on him.

Me: . . .

Why?

Kodiak: Because.

Me: Tell me.

Kodiak: I was mad it wasn't me.

Okay?

But it doesn't matter now,

does it?

You're into him, right?

Me: What about Liv?

Kodiak: What about her?

Me: I heard what she said to you last night.

The thing about doors staying open?

Kodiak: Oh.

Yeah.

It's not what you think.

I was talking to her about you.

It's like walking outside
at midnight
in summer.
It feels like night,
and anywhere else
it would look like night.
But in Alaska
it looks midday.

The sun sits high above the mountains,
and people are bicycling down the street.
A hot dog vender on the corner
is still up
selling reindeer sausages.

It never feels quite right,
or makes much sense.
Kodiak says with his words
that we shouldn't kiss,
but he doesn't want someone else to kiss me either.

I'm so angry.
So tired
of not knowing where people stand.
Why people do
the things they do

instead of saying
the things they feel.

This time,
it's me,
knocking on Mom's door.

She folds laundry
in little Marie Kondo piles,
organizing clothes by color
and size
and type.

"I need to know why.
Why you slept with Jack
when you loved Dad."

*Why did I kiss Fletcher
when I like Kodiak?*

She almost stops breathing,
clutching one of Dad's shirts
to her heart.
"I don't know."

I guess that's the answer.
She doesn't know,
and neither do I.

I guess we're not so different anyhow.

To: Cordelia Koenig (koenig.cordelia@tchs.edu)
From: Vidya Nadeer (nadeer.vidya@tchs.edu)
Subject: Pages

Cordelia,

I haven't received your last two poetry assignments.

Also checking in to see how things are going with your project and if you need any guidance. I'd like to see what you have been working on so I can help to make sure you're giving this project your very best. If you need anything, let me know. Please, take my advice and don't wait until the last minute to complete your project.

Vidya Nadeer

If I mess up
and don't do my best,
Ms. Nadeer could fail me.

If she fails me,
my early acceptance means nothing
and I'll have nowhere to go next year
because I won't be a high school graduate.

I tell myself
there are bigger things happening
than high school,
but really,
this is important.

I need to get back to the project,
find which part of this defines me
        Jack
        this thing with Kodiak
        Poetry
even if it derails me.

GeneQuest
Genetic Family Conversations

To: Jack Bisset *(online)*
From: Cordelia Koenig *(online)*

Sorry I wasn't around this weekend.

I've been thinking a lot. Talking to you, finding out about you, has been amazing. I always felt like there was something off about me, and that I didn't belong, and I really think you get that. Maybe this whole time I've been trying to fit in with my family because there's a whole part of myself I haven't been able to access. Really, what it all comes back to is that I didn't know you were my father.

I think that if we met, I might feel better, somehow.

Like a chapter of my life can finally open.

What do you think? Can we meet? Could you come up here?

Cordelia

He doesn't reply.
One hour.
Then two.
By the third
I've stopped what I'm doing
to stalk his Instagram.

I hover over the Follow button
like I'm willing it to reach him
so he responds
before I have to make contact
again.

I want to hear the ping of my phone
more than I want anything.
It doesn't matter that Sana texts
or Kodiak sent me a message
with pages
I'm supposed to read.
I just want Jack
to say yes.

I press Follow,
and instantly
he follows back.

The best stories aren't the ones on Instagram.
They're the ones in my mind.
Like the time I was little
and wanted to go see my favorite band live.
He knew a guy,
a friend of a friend,
who recorded an album with him.

He took me.
I was so little I couldn't see over the crowd,
but he put me on his shoulders,
and I tickled behind his ears
during my favorite song.
He pretended
he was going to drop me
and I screamed.

We laughed.
And laughed.
And laughed.

And I'll never forget
this memory that didn't happen.

@Jack_Bisset_band

Me: Hey.

Jack: Hi.

Sorry I didn't message you back earlier.

Me: I get it.

That's too much, right?

Maybe I should have waited to ask.

Jack: No.

It's not like that.

Coming up would be a lot. You know?

I left and I didn't ever think I'd come back.

Me: I get it. I'm sorry.

Jack: Listen.

There's no reason to be sorry.

Me: I don't want things to be weird. I like getting to know you.

Jack: I like that too. And I do want to meet you.

I've thought a lot about how that would look.

Me: How do you think it would look?

Jack: Well.

If you came here, we'd start the day off at Pike Place.

Have you ever been?

Me: No!

Jack: We'd go there and see the wharf.

There's also this gross bubble gum wall you should check out.

Kids love it.

A few years ago I did a photo shoot there with a band I worked with.

Me: That sounds amazing.

Jack: Then we'd hit up Beecher's Cheese for lunch.

And I'd show you the very first Starbucks.

Me: I can do coffee!!!!

Jack: I'd take you to my studio.

Show you what it looks like.

And how it works.

Me: What if I could do that?

Come to Seattle?

Jack: That would be amazing.

Me: I have enough in my bank account right now.

I just looked at tickets.

Jack: Oh kid. I don't know.

Me: Why? Don't you want to meet me?

Jack: I do, but it's complicated.

Have you talked to your mom about this?

And your dad. Wouldn't it hurt his feelings?

Wouldn't it hurt his feelings?

I can't say
he doesn't know.

Or since when did you care about his feelings?

The man who has been here
for eighteen years
and held my hand
and taught me how to ride a bike
kissed my boo-boos
and read *The Tempest*
until I fell asleep.
Who picked me up
when I was too drunk.
Who loves me.

Doesn't know.

Things I would have missed if Dad wasn't my dad:

Yearly Shakespeare festival we all complain about going
to but secretly love
His go-to "breakfast for dinner" meal. It's the best.
All his jokes and quotes
His NPR marathons
Iris

@Jack_Bisset_band

Jack: Cordelia.

Does your dad know?

Me: Not exactly.

But it's okay.

If we met—it would be okay.

My mom wouldn't care.

We'd figure it out.

Jack: *Message not received.*

Me: Jack?

Jack: *Message not received.*

Me: What happened?

Jack: *Message not received.*

He blocked me.

The man
I share blood with
blocked me.

I'm shaking,
my fingers so tight
against my phone
I'm scared
I'll shatter the screen.

My stomach
drops.
The sickening
thud
as it settles
too low
to scream.

why
Why
WHY

Outside my window
on the street
in the yard
are leaves
matted
left over
from last year's autumn.

They were bright orange last year
before the snow and ice
now they're a moldy brown color
like my hair.

I'm crying soft tears,
wishing winter could come back,
when Dad walks in
and holds me
without talking
for a long time.

How fucked up is it?

Dad is holding me,
listening to my sobs,
and drying my tears

because my birth father,
the one he doesn't know about,
blocked me.

Did Dad console Mom when she left Jack?
Did he hold her this way
and let her break?
And when he asked what was wrong,
did she lie the way I did and say,
"It's just this project.
It's too hard."

This isn't what I thought
or ever imagined
this would be like.

How could I know
what I would tumble into?
Who I would learn about?

"Oh honey."
He brushes hair
from my face.
"Why don't you talk to Bea?
I know how she can be sometimes,

but she means well.
She had the hardest time
when she was doing hers."

"This is different,"
I promise.

"It's not.
Finding yourself,
it's hard
no matter what you learn.
I'm still trying to find myself.
In every play I read
every book I scour
every class I teach
I'm searching for an answer
to a question
I don't know how to ask.
Same with your mom,
she's searching for herself
in her own way too.
Talk to her,
she wants to talk to you."

"I can't."

"Why is it all my girls struggle with their mom?
Someday, she'll be your best friend."

Masks I currently wear:

- School Mask that says I'm fine. I'm ready for college, and I'm not scared.
- Jack Mask that says that I'm mature and cool, and ready to meet him.
- Dad Mask that says I don't spend every day thinking about how he isn't my real dad.
- Sana Mask that says there's nothing I've ever hidden from you.
- Kodi Mask that says I understand him. I'm cool. I'm mature. I play these games all the time.

Sister Bea

Me: Can we talk?

Bea: Sure.

Me: Without you getting upset or acting like I'm a little
kid and I don't know what I'm talking about?

Bea: I'm not sure what you mean by that.

But yeah.

Me: I'm having a hard time with my project.

Dad said you had a hard time too.

Bea: I did.

It was hard to find myself in people that aren't "real."

Most of them are just names with no faces.

So I dove in deeper and deeper.

I became obsessed.

I was on GeneQuest and AncestorHunt all the time.

But after I found out we were related to Emmeline
Pankhurst it clicked for me.

Me: You felt like what you found defined you?

Bea: Absolutely.

Me: To the point that it changed you?

Bea: For sure.

I guess it made me want to explore feminism more.

Actually, it's a big part of the reason I chose Brown.

Because they have an incredible Women's Studies

program.

Me: But you changed your major.

Bea: Yeah.

I did.

I don't want to be an academic for the rest of my life.

And Finance allows me stability later on.

What better way to be a feminist than to take charge of your own success?

Me: Yeah. I get that.

Bea: It's like this.

You've always had this connection with Dad, right?

Me: I have?

Bea: Yeah.

You've got that poet/artsy vibe thing.

And I've always connected with Mom on that "I want to take over the world" thing.

We're both workaholics.

Very Emmeline Pankhurst about things.

Me: Ah.

Bea: But on Dad's side we're actually related to Emily Dickinson.

God, have you done any of the AncestorHunt research or did you just log your ethnicities and call it a day?

Me: I guess the latter.

What does Iris get from our parents?

Bea: I think she's got a little bit of both.

Ever notice how she won't talk to people when she's mad?

Like Mom?

But she's got Dad's sense of humor.

Me: What if you didn't learn all this from your project?
What if what you learned changed everything you knew
but in a bad way?

Bea: What do you mean?

Me: I don't know.

Sorry.

Just having a bad night.

I'll talk to you soon. Okay?

Bea: Okay.

No.
You
are related to Emily Dickinson.

I'm related to a guy
in Seattle
with a tattoo
and a guitar
and a lot of story
who won't talk to me.

My creative line
is birthed from a different stream.
Like an imposter
floating toward the mouth
of a river
I don't belong in.

To: Cordelia Koenig (koenig.cordelia@tchs.edu)
From: Vidya Nadeer (nadeer.vidya@tchs.edu)
Subject: Conference

Cordelia,

I wanted to check in about a few things.

First, I'm putting together a list of students going to the conference with me in just two weeks! Have you thought more about attending? I really think you would enjoy it, and we'd love to have you along. I'll attach the necessary forms to this email in case.

Also, how is your project going? Did you receive my last email? I tried reaching out to you after class yesterday, but you've been leaving so quickly these days. I miss our post-third-period chats about what you are reading. I understand projects like this can be hard, and I want to make sure you're getting the help you need. Please let me know what sort of assistance I can offer.

Vidya Nadeer
Attached document: conferencepermissionslip.doc
Attached document: conferencestudentagreement.doc
Attached document: conferencescheduleandinfo.doc

Progress: to move forward

I am moving forward
and backward
at the same time.

Treading a snow-topped mountain
only to see
there is no safe route
for return.

Kodiak Jones

Me: Okay.

We need to get together.

Not like together-together.

Like lunch and poetry together.

Kodiak: Is this the nerd girl's version of Netflix and Chill?

Me: I'm being serious!

Ms. Nadeer emailed me last night asking for progress.

And I still haven't written a thing for this project.

Kodiak: You've been writing!

What about the poems that you showed me?

Me: Yeah.

I'm not going to air my family's dirty laundry in my senior project.

Can I come over and work on pages with you?

Like

Right now?

Kodiak: I thought you'd never ask.

I haven't seen Kodiak's parents in months,
but it feels like yesterday
that our families
saw each other
so often
we didn't have to ask questions
like
"How have you been?"

His mom hugs me,
warm and a little too long.
I ache
knowing she might know more about me
than I'm ready for her to know.

"We're headed out."
she says, jingling keys
and clutching a water bottle.
"Five-mile hike.
Be good."

Kodiak pulls his hat over his ears,
rolling his eyes on his way downstairs
to his room for me to follow.

Things going through my head:

- I'm about to be in Kodiak's room.
- With him.
- While his parents are gone.
- What did he mean when he said he was mad at himself?
- Is he going to try to kiss me?
- Do I want to kiss him? (Of course I do.)
- My heart already knows him.
- Even if everything is so messed up, I know him.

"They must trust you. A lot."
Kodiak points upstairs
where the sound of his mom closing the door
reverberates through the whole house
making me suddenly aware
that my skin
is tingling.
"They've never left me alone with a girl.
Especially after last year.
Liv and I—"

He looks over at the couch,
in the corner
of his room
probably remembering being
tangled up with Liv
the way
he thumbs his guitar strings.

Liv was unruly,
unkempt,
unavoidable.
She filled up a room,
with her loud voice
and purple hair
the way she filled his heart.

I'll never
be the girl
who fills up a room.

Kodiak must see something change
because he leans in, putting his hand on my knee
and whispering,
"What's wrong?"

My heart
I want to be free too.
Unkempt and unruly the way it might have been
if my "Maybe" life had happened.

I'm so tired of safety.
Of wearing the life vest,
and doing the right thing.
Playing moments like this in my head.
Wondering if Kodiak
would love the version of me
who grew up strumming Jack's guitar
instead of reciting Shakespeare.

Just for today,
I want to be the girl who grew up
unruly

unafraid
free.

I turn into Kodiak.
I pull him close
and press my lips to his
before I can think
of all the reasons
I
should
not.

Kissing Kodiak
is like opening a book.
The way his bottom lip drops
ever so slightly,
like I've tempted the spine apart.

Then my fingers linger
along the side of his arm,
tickling the surface of his skin
as if I'm keeping track of my spot.

How his pace quickens,
my pulse throbbing
against his touch—
heart pounding,
mind racing,
straight to the point in the book
where I want to stay up all night
trapped in its pages,
until there's nothing left.

It's the bookmark he places,
when he comes up for air,
breathless,
my mouth swollen

from the stubble on his face,
while we're tangled like a pretzel in his bed.

He pulls away,
kissing my eyelashes
and says, "You surprise me,
Cordelia Bedelia.
You always surprise me."

GeneQuest
Genetic Family Conversations

To: Jack Bisset *(unavailable)*
From: Cordelia Koenig *(online)*

Jack,

I think I freaked you out, and I'm sorry.

It's weird. I spent my whole life thinking I was supposed to be this one way because of how I was raised. Now, it's like I've discovered a whole new side to myself, and I want to know more. I feel like if I met you, it would help explain things I've always wondered about.

I'm not mad that you blocked me on Instagram. I get it.
I should have been honest from the start.

Please, just think about meeting.

Cordelia

GeneQuest
Genetic Family Conversations

To: Cordelia Koenig *(online)*
From: GeneQuest *(donotreply@genequest.com)*

The following email could not be sent.
This user no longer exists.

To: Jack Bisset (unavailable)
From: Cordelia Koenig (online)

Jack,

I think I freaked you out, and I'm sorry.

It's weird. I spent my whole life thinking I was supposed to be this one way because of how I was raised. Now, it's like I've discovered a whole new side to myself, and I want to know more. I feel like if I met you, it would help explain things I've always wondered about.

I'm not mad that you blocked me on Instagram. I get it.
I should have been more honest from the start.

Please, just think about meeting.

Cordelia

Jack Bisset

Me: Did you actually delete your GeneQuest account?

Sana-Friend ♥

Me: I am finally writing again!

Sana: Yeah? Was it about surprising me by outlining this stupid project?

Me: Uh. No. Poems.

Sana: Srsly.

You were right. Maddy is really awesome at helping with the written portion.

She wants me to write an outline today.

I shit you not.

Meanwhile, my soccer protégé down the street is moving.

So no more protégé.

Me: Wow.

What are you going to do?

Sana: No idea.

I'm screwed.

UNLESS . . .

Maybe you could ask Iris to come over and record a few videos. I don't think I have many left.

Me: Yeah. Sure.

Sana: What'd you do today?

That wasn't helping me with my project?

Me: I went to Kodiak's.

Sana: Yeah you did. 😊

Me: Come on . . .

It's not like that.

He's my partner.

Sana: Dude. I get it.

If Emma Fucking Daniels started knocking down my
door

I'd be all over her too.

Now that you're not . . .

Preoccupied

Wanna come hang out and we can work on stuff
together?

Me: Yes! I'll be right over.

Kodiak Jones

Kodiak: Well that was an entirely ineffective work
session.
Me: What?!
How?
I'm feeling incredibly inspired.
Kodiak: 😐
Me: I'm actually writing right now.
A real poem.
Kodiak: It's been that hard lately?
Me: Yeah.
I feel stuck.
Like before all this
everything I wrote about was just emotional.
Emo teenager stuff.
But this thing with my DNA—it's bigger.
Kodiak: If that happened to me I don't know what I'd do.
Me: It certainly feels like a crisis of character.
Question.
Do you feel like your ancestry shapes you?
Or the way you were raised?
Kodiak: My situation is completely different.
Me: I know.
Just answer.
Kodiak: Yeah.

At least on my mom's side.

They're Tlingit.

My ancestors share this history. A story.

Stories.

Basically my whole project is how that shared history was passed down generationally.

And trying to keep it alive in a fresh new way.

Me: What if you didn't know all those stories?

Wouldn't that be sad?

Kodiak: Yeah.

Me: I want to meet my dad.

Kodiak: I get that.

Me: It's hard because I know he's scared too.

And all the way in Seattle.

Kodiak: It's not that far.

Me: It's far enough to be a mess.

My DAD dad doesn't know, remember?

Kodiak: Okay.

I hesitate to say this.

Only because I've been trying to keep my shenanigans to a minimum.

And there are all sorts of ways this can make it even more complicated.

But you do know the poetry conference is in Seattle right?

Me: It is?

Kodiak: Do you even read those emails anymore that Ms. Nadeer sends?

Me: Yeah, I should do that.

Kodiak: Well. If you're going to go you better hurry. The deadline for the permission slips and paperwork is tomorrow morning.

Sister Bea

Bea: Hey.

Hello?

Okay. I guess you're not talking to me?

When you get this, call me.

To: Cordelia Koenig (koenig.cordelia@tchs.edu)
From: Vidya Nadeer (nadeer.vidya@tchs.edu)
Subject: Re: Conference

Dear Ms. Nadeer,

Please consider me as a definite go on the conference. I'll fill out the proper paperwork tonight and make sure to get it to you right away. While the poetry contest at the end sounds appealing, I do not think I'll have anything prepared enough.

Also, I am sending some of the poems I've been working on lately. It's not much, but it's all I have. I assure you that my project will display my best work and be completed on time.

Sincerely,

Cordelia Koenig

Jack Bisset

Me: Completely unrelated but I'm coming to Seattle. I still want to meet if you're up for it. Let me know!

Sana-Friend ♥

Me: Okay.

When I get there I need to borrow your internet stalking
skills.

Sana: Oh honey . . .

If you think for a second I haven't already internet
stalked the SHIT out of Kodiak you're cray.

Me: What?

Sana: Wait.

That's not who you want me to stalk?

Me: No . . .

But what did you find?

Sana: Wait.

Only if we stop saying stalk.

I'll never fulfill my ambition of being Veronica Mars
if I don't stop saying "stalk" and totally legitimize myself
by saying "investigate."

Me: Okay. INVESTIGATE.

Sana: So who?

Me: My biological father.

Sana: Oh shit.

Me: Yeah.

Sana: What do you want to know?

Me: Address?

Place of employment?

I know he works at a music studio in Seattle.

But that's it.

Sana: Uhhhh.

Delia?

This feels a little weird.

Me: I know. Trust me?

It's important.

Sana: Can't you ask him where he works?

Me: No.

Sana: All right.

Come over.

I'll stalk him.

And you can do my project.

Me: IF I CAN'T CALL IT STALKING YOU CAN'T CALL IT STALKING!

Past the waterlogged soccer fields
just beyond the highway
lined with spring-cleanup trash bags
is Sana's trailer
that feels like home.

All warm,
without heat.
The raindrops hitting the roof
make pinging sounds that remind me
my ears still hear the world beyond
the voice in my head that says,
You don't belong, and you never will.

Sana's trailer says otherwise.
It whispers:
You fit perfectly.
In Sana's room
sitting on her bed,
just a mattress
flopped on the floor,
littered with pillows.

Here
I don't have to pretend I don't know.
That I have been ignoring Bea,

while Jack ignores me.
Or pretending Mom isn't falling apart,
drinking too many glasses of wine at dinner.
Or pretending not to see
the way Dad looks down at his plate too
like he's trying to rearrange the table
to fit us all.

Sana hugs me
and whispers,
"Tell me everything, Cordelia.
I know something is wrong."
I hug her back
and spill

E
V
E
R
Y
T
H
I
N
G.

How I talked to Jack.
How it felt like my whole life
was leading up to finding him.

How he disappeared as soon as I said I wanted to meet.
How I knew it was because he was scared.
That maybe seeing me was too much for him,
because it all felt like too much for me too.

How it hurt so badly
to think he needed to cut me out
when I just wanted to know him.

I tell her I booked a ticket to Seattle.
I forged my parents' signatures on the permission slip,
but I'll tell them later.
If I can figure out where Jack lives
I might be able to see him while I'm there.
Then maybe I'll know who I am.

I tell her about Kodiak.
How my heart already knows him,
and when we kissed
and pretzeled
and touched
I felt free.

Alive.

Like it was supposed to be that way.
Even though I know she worries about me
and she's scared I'll get hurt
or pregnant
or whatever,
this is what I want.

And I know they're both crazy things.
That I want to meet Jack.
That I want to be with Kodiak.
But I can't help what my heart feels
No matter how silly.
This.
Is.
What.
I.
Need.

"Fucksticks.
Why didn't you tell me this before?"
Sana reaches for my hand.

"Because,"
I say,
"How could you understand?
I don't even understand."

"If anyone gets daddy issues,
it's me."

"It's different.
Your dad died when you were little,
my mom kept mine from me."

"Delia," she starts,
but I cut her off.
I feel my nose pinch
tears trailing down my cheeks
like the raindrops on her roof.

"And the Kodiak thing.
If you think he's bad,
how can I like him this much?"

"Oh Cordelia.

My beautiful, sweet friend.

Don't you see it has nothing to do with not liking him?

Dude. Kodiak is awesome.

I get the appeal.

But I'm worried for you.

You may have grown up together

but you're from very different worlds.

And I'm scared you can't see

that even if he's not bad

it doesn't mean he's good for you.

But see,

it's not just Kodiak—

I don't think any guy is good enough for you."

Missed call from Mom- 6:17 pm

Missed call from Mom- 6:49 pm

Text from Mom- Honey.

We need to talk.

Where are you?

Missed call from Dad- 6:57 pm

Missed call from Mom- 7:20 pm

Text from Kodiak- Your mom is looking for you.

She called my mom.

Are you okay?

Missed call from Mom- 7:24 pm

Missed call from Mom- 7:24 pm

Text from Bea- Not that you'll respond, but Mom just texted me.

She's worried about you.

Call her back when you get a second.

And while you're at it, call me back.

I really need to talk to you about something.

Missed call from Mom- 7:24 pm

Text from Mom- Cordelia.

I'm starting to get worried.

Mom

Me: Hey

Sorry

Sana and I were hanging out.

My phone was on Silent.

Mom: Oh.

Okay.

You need to come home.

We got an email from Ms. Nadeer.

Apparently we signed a permission slip last night?

Me: I can explain.

To: Cordelia Koenig (CordeliaBedelia99@gmail.com)
From: Julie Koenig (koenig@aurorarealestate.com)
Subject: Fwd: Pacific Northwest Young Poets Conference

Look familiar?

To: Julie Koenig (koenig@aurorarealestate.com)
From: Vidya Nadeer (nadeer.vidya@tchs.edu)
Subject: Pacific Northwest Young Poets Conference

Dear Julie and Andrew,

I'm so pleased that Cordelia decided to come to the conference. I've brought it up many times this semester because I truly feel she will get so much from it. Thank you for supporting her in her craft and completing the necessary documents so quickly.

Soon I'll be sending a detailed parent email about what to expect that includes a more specific schedule of our events there this year, including the spoken word contest on the last day. But the conference will be a long-weekend conference. We will arrive in Seattle very early on a Friday morning and return late Sunday night. Best,

Vidya Nadeer

"Is this about him?"
Dad asks.

My heart lingers in my chest,
the beat pounding in my ears
like ice-melt thrown on pavement
until he adds,

"Kodiak?"

"No.
No.
No."
I promise.
Mom is quiet,
looking out the window.
Dad has no quotes,
and he doesn't even try to joke.

"Honey,
you have to understand how this looks.
Ever since you've started hanging out with him,
you aren't the same.
You're forgetting your responsibilities,

you got drunk,
you don't check in.
Now you're forging our signatures?"

"It's not like that."

"Then tell us what it's like.
Why we should let you go
when you lied to your teacher
and committed a crime?"

I am too tired to pretend anymore.
"I don't know, Mom,
can you think of any reason I shouldn't go?"

Mom's eyes dart to me,
cold, icy crystals around the rims
that make me believe
for a moment
it's still winter.
"I'm not sure what you mean by that.
Do you want us to go with you?
Ms. Nadeer said there was some sort of
spoken word contest?"

I tell them I won't be performing any poem,
that there's no need for them to go.

It's not anger in her eyes I see,
and I realize,
it never was.

It was never that I was different
or she didn't understand me.

I've just always been
the evidence
of her lie
that could destroy
the staged home
we live in.

Sana-Friend ♥

Sana: Girl. Are you in some serious shit with your
parents?
I can't believe you forged their signatures.
Hooking up with a rebel
getting shit-faced at bonfires.
You've changed, Cordelia Ann Koenig.
Me: I don't know about serious shit.
Right now I'm sitting in my room.
Staring out the window.
At a moose.
While my parents have a chat to contemplate my
punishment.
Sana: Bitchin'
Me: My dad thinks I've changed.
Sana: See my above statement.
Me: Maybe change is a good thing?
Sana: As long as you don't lose the parts that make you
you.
You're pretty fucking awesome.
It would suck if you started to suck.

"Honey—
we talked for a long time over dinner
and decided to let you go.
After all,
in a few months,
you'll be adult enough
to make these choices
for yourself.

But it needs to stop:
the lying,
the sneaking.
Because we want to build
a trusting relationship
with you,
even if it means
you are honest
about how you feel
for that boy."

And Dad says it
so matter-of-factly
because he doesn't get it.
That mine are not the lies that hurt us;
mine are the lies that save us.

To: Cordelia Koenig (koenig.cordelia@tchs.edu)
From: Vidya Nadeer (nadeer.vidya@tchs.edu)
Subject: Poetry Contest

Cordelia,

I am thrilled you decided to join us on the conference trip. When I mentioned taking a group of students at the beginning of the year, we were working on our poetry unit, and I instantly thought of you. You have so much innate talent for verse, and I don't want you to sell yourself short because you feel unprepared.

Take it from me: there are many experiences I missed out on because I was too afraid to try. The last poem you sent, about nature versus nurture, was beautiful. I'd love to hear you perform that for the spoken word contest at the conference.

Please, just think about it.

Best,

Vidya Nadeer

Sana-Friend ♥

Sana: All right.

I did it.

I dug deep.

I might have done some of this illegally.

See: hacking

Me: Oh.

Don't tell me that.

Sana: Hey.

You wanted to be a badass.

Get all edgy.

I'm just helping the process along.

Me: Sweet.

Did you find his address?

Sana: Yeah.

So that's a thing.

Me: You couldn't find it?

Sana: Oh I found an address.

But I also Google Mapped the hell out of it.

His apartment location is sketchy AF.

Like a 24-minute walk to Pike Place Market. Which is a big deal in Seattle.

Or an 8-minute drive if you get a ride.

Me: Maybe it looks sketchy because it's in the city.

Sana: Bitch I know sketch when I see it.

Me: He's a music producer.
I bet the inside is super nice.
Sana: Be careful.

Information about Jack Bisset

Prepared by Sana Sasaki

(master ~~stalker~~ investigator)

Name: Jack Allan Bisset

DOB: July 9, 1973

Last known address:

2340 South Jefferson Street

Apartment 240

Seattle, WA 98104

(But sketchy AF)

Phone Number: 206-555-1232

Email Address: jackbisset73@gmail.com

Instagram: Jack_Bisset_band

Facebook:@jackyboybisset

Place of employment: Waterfront Studios (unverified)

Last verified place of employment: Rollin' with My Homies Smoke Shop (I wish that was a joke. He actually worked at a head shop. But that was three years ago. No idea what he's been up to since.)

Frequented establishments: Parkhill Bistro (Though if I'm being honest, pictures of this place look sketchier than the head shop! There's legit a bra hanging behind the bar and dollar bills covering the ceiling. My kind of establishment.)

He's taken a lot of pictures at Pike Place.

He also used to check in at a food truck called Pete's BBQ, but it's closed now.

Sana-Friend ♥

Sana: Okay.

It wasn't easy.

I had to crawl deep into the dark net.

Roll out some of my supersecret skills.

And against my better judgment I sent you all the info I could get.

Me: Thank you.

Sana: Also, did you ever ask Iris about soccer?

Me: Crap.

I did.

But she's supposed to talk to Mom about it.

Sorry—reading your notes on Jack.

Sana: Sketch sauce for sure.

Me: Are you sure this is the same guy?

Sana: Yep.

The only Jack Bisset in the greater Pacific Northwest.

And if you can't tell, I'm not 100% on board with you finding this dude.

Me: You don't say.

Sana: I think there's a lot you don't know about him.

What if he's dangerous?

More dangerous than a little dishonesty about his place of employment.

Me: He's my dad.

I know he wasn't lying about some of that stuff. Maybe what you found is old information.

Sana: You met the guy like two minutes ago.

Correction: You haven't EVEN met the guy.

He could be anyone.

And think about it.

Your mom probably kept you from knowing about him for a reason.

Me: Yeah, because she doesn't want my dad to know she screwed someone else.

Sana: Be careful.

Don't go finding this guy on your own.

Me: Yeah.

Okay.

Whatever.

To: Jack Bisset (jackbisset73@gmail.com)
From: Cordelia Koenig (CordeliaBedelia99@gmail.com)
Subject: Please read.

It's kind of weird, I know. But I found your email address.

I wasn't 100% honest about my parents being on board. But I'm going to be in Seattle this weekend for a school trip thing, and I still want to meet you. Even if it's just for lunch or something. And this time, my mom definitely knows.

Please.
Just think about it.

Cordelia

I'm packing my bags
paying close attention
to each outfit
that might be
the outfit
I wear
when I meet
Jack.

Iris trails in
bouncing a soccer ball
on her knee
even though it's not allowed
in the house
filled with lies.

"Sana said she texted you,"
Iris starts,
going on to reveal my lie.
I feel terrible.
I forgot.
I forgot
I completely forgot
I never asked her about Sana
and soccer.

"I miss you." Iris seems so small.
"I'm not gone yet," I say.
Then Iris puts her ball
on the ground
and lays her head on top
of my suitcase
like it might keep me here
a little longer.

"Don't be mad."
Her lip quivers,
"But you haven't really been here
in a long time.
I miss my sister."

I replay the last weeks
and all the ways
I've failed her.
I also forgot to pick her up.
Forgot she's here too
watching me
watch Mom
with an innocent set of eyes.

I finally pull my gaze to hers
and soften, trading the luggage tag
for a strand of her hair.

"I'm sorry, Iris.
It's the project.
It changed everything."

"Then change the project."

To: Cordelia Koenig (koenig.cordelia@tchs.edu)
From: Vidya Nadeer (nadeer.vidya@tchs.edu)
Subject: Re: Poetry Contest

I really think you should contribute your poetry to the spoken word contest.

Just so you know, you can sign up right until the very end.

Best,

Vidya Nadeer

To: Sana Sasaki (sasakicentral@gmail.com)

From: Cordelia Koenig (CordeliaBedelia99@gmail.com)

Subject: Ms. Nadeer and her crazy ideas

All right—best friend.

The very first screener of my written words.

Most humble critic of every poem.

You get the point.

Ms. Nadeer, like, really wants me to submit a poem to this poetry contest in Seattle. I've been thinking about it, but I'm not sure. Can you read it and let me know what you think? Is this even worth trying to get entered?

Much love,

Cordelia

PS—Iris is a go on helping you with your project and said she'd text soon!

Attached document: seniorprojectproposal.doc

The flight check-in kiosks are barren
in the middle of the night.
Mom stands in front of me
like she's not sure if she should hug me
or hit me.

My classmates and Ms. Nadeer are ahead
tossing their luggage onto the belt.
I run my fingers along the strap of my bag
wondering what
if anything
to say.

"Are you going to spend time with him?"
Mom chews the corners of her gnawed nails,
looking between me
and Kodiak, who is checking his bags.

I stare back at him,
printing his tickets,
and he waves
all open and eagle.

I shrug,
wondering how
the weight of the mountains,

their growing shadows,
has suffocated us.
Even if I didn't think she understood
at least we used to be able to talk.

"That's not who I mean."
She's looking at me
looking at Kodiak.
I checked up on him too, you know.
He's in Seattle."
The corner of her mouth twists
and she drags a bloody nail against her lip.
They're worse than they were before.

He is between us again. Jack.

"What do you think, Mom? Would you?"

As the flight attendant's voice
crackles overhead
I shove my phone in my bag
ignoring yet another call from Bea.
Kodiak grabs my hand
and draws a heart in my palm,
and for a second,
I forget.

Like he's connecting us
again.
Making our
side-by-side seats
a love seat.

I whisper to him
that I am afraid,
and he leans in
until our foreheads touch,
and I can feel
his breath
filling my lungs
reminding me
to breathe.

"This big thing
doesn't define you.
Only you
control
what makes you
who you are."

He's wrong,
but I don't argue.
Instead I rest my head
on his shoulder,
where it belongs.
And listen,
as we take off
for a 3.5-hour flight,
while he recites
the words
he says
my heart gave him.

The last things I hear as I fall asleep:

- The hum of a jet taking off.
- Kodiak's notebook opening.
- Paper rustling as he rips the staples from the pages.
- His voice quiet.
- Timid.

"I was born Eagle,
my name is for Bear,
but I feel like my soul
belongs to Raven."

When you're trapped in a hotel
everything is
tiny soaps
tiny shampoos
tiny pockets of time
to sneak away.

It's awkward glances in the elevator,
missed opportunities with mentors
because you're picking at a continental breakfast
wondering how long Ms. Nadeer is going to watch you
and if you can get to South Jefferson Street
before anyone notices.

I'm missing the first day of the conference
and everything it should be—
trading breakout sessions for maps
poems for public transit routes
people with passion so strong in their bones
you want to trap their words in your heart
and tether yourself to their memories:
for a person who might not even want to see me.

Kodiak Jones

Kodiak: Which breakout are you doing next?

Me: I don't know.

Wanna skip with me? 😈

Kodiak: I'd love to

but I really want to hit this next session.

There's one about slam poetry I need to check out.

I just went to a practice session for the spoken word

contest.

I'm nervous.

Me: I'm afraid I'll run out of time.

And every minute I'm not trying to meet him

Is a minute I haven't met him.

Kodiak: I know.

But we just got here.

I don't want to miss out on this stuff tho.

My parents had to scrounge to get me here.

You know?

Me: I get it.

And you're right.

I shouldn't ask you to leave when it's not your deal.

Maybe I'll go on my own.

Kodiak: Wait.

Don't do that.

What about tomorrow?

We're supposed to go to Pike Place. Doesn't he live close to there?

Me: How did you know that?

Kodiak: You told me.

Didn't you?

Me: I don't remember telling you.

Kodiak: You're probably tired.

Meet me at the slam poetry session?

Me: Yeah.

Sure.

Sana-Friend ♥

Me: Hey.

I'm losing my mind.

I think I'm going to text Jack.

Hey.

Are you there?

Seattle smells
like exhaust puffing
and coffee brewing on every street,
with a lurking fish-stench
like Seward.
Only bigger.

And still,
the sweet scent of trees somewhere behind the city,
like an aftertaste.

Seattle feels
like it might have once been home.
Maybe it's my heart that already knows this place
because Jack calls it home.

Ms. Nadeer walks along curbs and points out street art
she says she loves.
Her dark eyes are lighter in the city,
like she feels at home here too
the way I feel alive in my poetry
or listening to Kodiak play guitar.
There's a gravity to Seattle
I can't ignore.
I can't even enjoy it,
because I'm busy wondering

if Jack is on the next street,
and what would happen if
we bumped into him.

As we turn down Stewart Street,
then Post Alley,
she says,
"When I first came to Seattle
I was a young girl,
and Pike Place
felt magical.
It's still my favorite destination."

This is where Jack would've brought me
if we ever got
the day we planned
the way we planned it.
And I feel cheated,
knowing I won't get this
with him.

Kodiak and I linger at the end of the group,
our held hands between us
as I check my phone's map.
Not for the destination of our makeshift tour
but for Jack's house—
and my breakaway moment.

While our class is gathered,
watching men yell and throw fish,
I pull Kodiak
by the hand,
slipping down a
crowded
surging alley between market stalls
and people
traveling in every direction.

We sneak away,
stealing kisses along the way,
down a set of concrete stairs.
A smile crinkles
into the corners of his eyes
when I catch him muttering
—trying to memorize—
his poem beneath his breath.

"You'll do great," I say,
trying not to look at my phone.

"I really need the extra credit."

I think back to what Sana said
—how she heard he might be back
next year too.
And like he might realize he said
too much.
"You ready?" he asks,
whispering lips
on mine.

He stops at the bottom of the stairs,
set in front of a wall,
with gum stuck to every surface.
Thousands of colors,
fill the space.
It would've been pretty
like a Pollock painting
if it wasn't so gross.

The wall Jack
promised in his messages.

Kodiak kisses me again.
I want to feel the free fall I felt
the day we kissed at his house,
but my stomach quivers.
I don't have time.
Pulling away,
I show him the address in my phone.

"This is my only chance.
Tomorrow is Sunday,
our last full day.
Today we have to
find my father."

"You're shaking," Kodiak whispers.
"Maybe we shouldn't do this."

He's right.
The quivering in my stomach
now extends through my entire body,
the reverberation
loosens my soul.

I'm so close to seeing Jack.
A twenty-five-minute half-run from the gum wall,
then I'll have an in-person idea
of what my father looks like.
See if his smile is crooked
like mine,
or if he's got long ears
and a single dimple.
Kodiak puts his arm around me,
pulling me close,
and we walk in tandem
as if we've done this before.

He's wrong about one thing.
We have to do this.

"We have to do this."
I take a few steps
before I realize
Kodiak stopped.

"Doesn't he know we're coming?"
he asks.

"He stopped answering my emails."
I say,
"But what does it matter?"

"It matters."
Kodiak's voice changes,
it's strained,
and something flickers in his eyes
that feels like anger.

"No."
I grit my teeth and
in a voice that matches his anger:
"I was ready to do this yesterday.
Over and done.
I waited for *you*.

"I can't do this without you."

"Listen—" he starts,
voice not raised
but shoulders straight.
"I've been supportive this entire time.
I've got a lot at risk.
Cordelia, I'm still on probation.
If I get caught—

"I'm worried this won't
be what you think it is.
If I learned anything with Liv
it's that you can't force a relationship
to be something it isn't."

I start to shake all over again,
finding too much truth
in his words.

"Maybe I'm wrong."
I try to find something to look at.
The street.
The signs.
The sky.
"But I'll never know if I don't go."

Then the anger in his eyes
seems to melt
like ice cream
losing form.
It's replaced with something
I don't quite know.
Something
that makes me feel
like he sees something
he didn't before.
"You're right."

We cross a busy street
our shoulders too close
to everyone
who doesn't belong
in my story.

Kodiak leads,
headfirst now,
like he can't wait
to end this detour
when I want to go slow.

So when I meet my dad,
for the first time,
I can remember his cologne.
And the way his tattoo looks in person.
How his voice sounds
when it's not muffled
behind the static
of our phones.

When we march up the stairs
to Apartment 240
of a building that feels
all wrong

I freeze,
remembering what Sana said
about being careful.

A baby screams
somewhere nearby.
An ashtray sits outside the door
on a peeling windowsill,
and my stomach lurches at
the scent of stale beer
wafting from inside.

It is all wrong—
snow in July,
Halloween candy in summer.
A thaw come too early,
the hibernating bears
who aren't ready.

This isn't the way I'm supposed to meet my father.

"You good?"
Kodiak asks,
studying every disgusting detail
with his eagle eyes.

Long enough
to maybe change my mind.

Kodiak knocks for me.

A woman answers the door.
I recognize her,
instantly:
one of Jack's Instagram women.

Only her hair isn't silky smooth,
the bright red dress in pictures
replaced
with a bleach-stained shirt
and cutoff jeans.

She's popping gum
between nicotine-stained teeth
looking at me
with her arms crossed,
eyes narrowed
like she can't understand
what I'm possibly
here for.

"What do you want?"

"I'm looking for Jack Bisset," I say.

She actually scoffs,
picking one of the cigarette butts

out of the ashtray
lighting the end
to inhale one last drag.

Her eyes go all misty,
Sad.
Mad.
Hurt.
Angry.
Confused.
"I haven't seen that piece of shit
since he walked out
a few weeks ago."

My heart's sinking faster
than our shuffle back down the stairs,
swollen with disbelief and relief.

She calls down to us:

"Might want to try Parkhill Bistro."
The place in Sana's email.
"Last I heard he got a gig there,
if he hasn't fucked it up already."

I expected a home,
maybe a girlfriend,
in some fancy apartment
that overlooks Puget Sound.
So high it makes you dizzy
when you get close enough
to the window's edge.

I expected a tour of the city,
a day at his office,
watching bands I don't know
make music only a few people care about
in a sound room
commanded by his hands.

I expected a connection.
Our eyes would meet
and I'd see part of me.
Like we both hate sushi,
but love Chinese,
and think poems are the music
that connects word to sound.
He has to say something
a million times in his heart
before he says it with his tongue.

And he loves fiercely
the same way I need to be loved.

I still expect those things.

I
Never
Thought
It
Would
Hurt
This
Bad.

I don't know what's worse:
the heat of Kodiak's gaze on me
or the rib-crushing embarrassment.
The way my chest feels hollow,
empty like the promises Jack made.

My mother's words
over and over in my head:
He's not a good guy.

It can't be right.
I didn't come this far,
sneak away from the group,
and lie to my father
to uncover the lies
of my other father.

Kodiak brushes the tears from my cheeks
and kisses the side of my face.
"Don't cry, Del.
He doesn't deserve your tears."

"Let's go to Parkhill.
One more stop, just one."
If I can get there,
if I can see him,
he can explain
what doesn't
make sense.

Will any of this ever make sense?

Vidya Nadeer, Kodiak Jones

Vidya Nadeer: Where are you?

Seems as though you've been separated from the group.

I need one of you to text me back immediately.

Kodiak: Sorry.

We got lost.

Me: Headed back now!

Where are you?

Vidya Nadeer: Meeting at the pier.

I expect you here shortly.

The pier smells like the oddest combination
of sweet flowers
and salty fish,
puckered together
and lingering long after you leave.

Our classmates take selfies in front of
a brand-new ocean.
They get to put everything from Tundra Cove
out of their minds—
Their Seattle selves laugh freely
but I cry timid tears into Kodiak's shoulder
because I'll never be free like the eagle
or strong like the bear.

Ms. Nadeer dips her glasses on her face,
making sure we see she notices us.
A self-conscious bubble settles
somewhere between my throat
and stomach.

I slip my hand out of Kodiak's,
rubbing it against my pants,
the way I wish I could wipe away this memory.

Jack Bisset

Me: I know I'm blocked everywhere else, and you aren't going to respond to this text either. I tried going to the address I had for you. I met a woman there who said you don't live there anymore. I don't understand, but I want you to know that even if you aren't who you said you are, it doesn't change anything for me. I leave late tomorrow night/early Monday morning and I'm staying at the DoubleTree closest to the airport.

Jack: I can't.

Me: Please.

Jack: *error*

Me: Just for a few minutes.

Jack: *error*

Me: I want to meet you.

Jack: *error*

Kodiak Jones

Me: What are you doing?

Kodiak: Lying in bed.

Carson is sneaking over to Vanessa and Lindsay's room as soon as Ms. Nadeer is done doing checks. Want to come with us?

Maybe get your mind off stuff.

Or you could come over here. 😊

Me: I have another idea.

Meet me by the pool?

Kodiak: Give me ten.

I beg Kodiak.
Just one more time.
One more time,
one more try,
so I can meet Jack.

"I came all this way,
and it will kill me
to leave
never knowing
what he looks like."

Without the filters,
without the text.
Or the apartment,
or job.

Then maybe I'll know what it was
that swept my mom away from my dad.

"Last time," I promise.

"Then we're done?"

Kodiak's words are tired,
I've heard them before.

Like a parent,
stretched thin
by a child
who wants too much.
"If we got caught I'd be done."

Done.
"Promise."

At night
the Seattle lights
don't seem as pretty
as they do in pictures.
The city doesn't look alive.
The Space Needle is too far
to bring comfort from familiarity.
I barely recognize its shape.
At least not in this little spot.
A seedy line of dive bars
and a homeless man who says,
"I'd like to kiss a girl like you," when I pass.
Kodiak holds my hand tighter.

It's not the man who might take me,
but the night itself,
pulsating with the lie I sold myself
that Jack is
something
he might not be.

I use the only-for-emergency credit card
to get a rideshare account.
Even then it still takes 27 minutes
to get to Parkhill.

A wave of people is leaving,
my stomach clenches,
eyeballing every man
for a tattoo on their collarbone
of a woman who looks
like my mother.

It's hazy outside the bar,
with a neon Open sign
hidden between ads for beer
and wine
and liquor.
A chalkboard promises the live music
I can already hear from the street.
A woman crooning
through crackled windpipes
sings an old country song.
A large man stands at the door,
checking IDs.

I point to him,
leaning into Kodiak
so I can take in the smell of home
instead of fear. Kodiak says,
"Go wait in the alley.

There's a back entrance and
I can come around and sneak you in."

It's dark,
and my heart pounds with every step I take
over broken glass
and a filmy liquid coating the ground.
The dumpster next to me stinks
of rotten food
and booze
and regret.
It makes me wonder if I made a mistake
until I see Kodiak through
a tiny side window.

He's effortless,
handing his ID off,
rubbing his chin
with the tips of his fingers,
smiling until his dimple shows.
I'm not the only one with masks.

He stops at the bar,
nodding to someone behind it
—is it *Jack?*—
before pointing a finger
like he's telling the bartender
which beer he wants.

Kodiak heads to the back
and I run
in rhythm with my heartbeat
to the back entrance.

He slips the door open,
pulling me out of the darkness
and guiding me through
to where my answers
must be.

The inside of Parkhill looks like any bar
in any movie
I've ever seen.

There are bright tin signs
covering every inch of wall.
My lungs tighten
when I look at the people drinking
expecting one of them to be Jack
but they're not.

Kodiak doesn't take his hand from my back
even as we approach the bartender,
who looks down at me,
confusion thread through her too-tweezed brows.

"Honey, whaddya need?"
A loaded question.

I ask if she knows Jack.
Does he work here?
Would he be around this weekend?

The confusion clears away,
making room for something else.
She and Kodiak share a glance,
and I feel my shoulders shudder against
his frame
as I see her shake her head back and forth.
Because I can't help it.
My body cries even when my eyes can't.

"He was bar-backing a few weeks ago.
Sweet pea, I don't know what you're doing
lookin' for him,
but it ain't gonna lead anywhere good.
You aren't..."
Her lips peel back uncomfortably.
"You're not in any sort of trouble,
are you?"

Her eyes move from me to Kodiak.
"You gotta get her outta here.
Can't have minors at the bar,
no matter who she's trying to find."

My whole body sags beneath my thin layer of skin,
the weight of the information
I already knew.

It was all a lie.
Every bit.
Every ounce of promise in his emails.
The job.
The apartment.
The life.
Was a lie.

And what's bigger—
the lie I told myself.
How everything would've been
if I'd grown up
strumming my fingers on his guitar,
tracing the lines of his tattoo,
and living in a different picture than the one I got.

The truth is:
I don't belong in that picture
any more than I belong in this one.

The stench wafting from the trash doesn't bother me,
and I don't feel myself clasping on to his arm.
Only the stinging pain radiating from my heart,
spreading into my fingertips.

"Are you okay?"
Kodiak asks,
catching me
before I drag my feet through
the broken glass underfoot.

"It'll never be okay,"
I say between sobs.
"I thought if I met him,
I could numb
the feeling
of not knowing."
That maybe,
there was a way to bring myself
peace
with what Mom tried to
forget-me-not
away.

He presses his forehead to mine,
sucking in a deep breath

as if trying to reason
something in himself.
He reaches into his pocket,
sliding his fake ID
between us.
"Let's turn this night around."

There's a shift in the air,
as a night breeze picks up,
to dry my tears.

Kodiak Jones smiles dangerously,
a glimmer of the boy he tried so hard to leave behind,
reminding me that before I came along
he was the one who was troubled.

After a stop at a sleazy liquor store
and a giddy walk back to the hotel,
I'm thankful for roommates who also
sneak out.

The first drink
mellows me enough
to giggle
and freely shift
into a place
inside Kodiak's arms.

The second drink
has me laughing
so light
I almost forget
my heart
is broken.

It's the third drink,
gulped down too quick.
My lips on his,
with the heat
between my legs
so warm
I don't know how

I went my entire life
never feeling this.

His hands
on me,
pulling my shirt
over my head.
That heat spreading
through my limbs,
my mouth hungrily kissing,
a completely opened book.

I ignore
the care of Kodiak's fingers
tangled in my hair.
The look in his eyes
that says he can't get enough—
until it's too late
to take anything back.

Kodiak Jones

> **Kodiak:** Please.
>
> Cordelia—
>
> Open the door.
>
> I look like an idiot out here in the hall texting when you can come out.
>
> And we can have a real conversation.
>
> **Me:** Go away.
>
> **Kodiak:** Come on.
>
> You know I can't do that.
>
> **Me:** Go.
>
> **Kodiak:** I didn't want your first time to be like this.
>
> I'm sorry.
>
> **Me:** What makes you think it's my first time?
>
> **Kodiak:** . . .

Sana-Friend ♥

Me: I need emotional support.

I've had a little bit to drink.

Sana: You're drunk.

Me: Yes.

I need my best friend.

Sana: Better go find Kodiak then.

Me: Can't.

I can't ever see him again.

Sana: Yeah?

Did you accidentally forward him your senior proposal project where he found out you requested specifically not to be his partner?

Oh wait.

That's me.

Me: Sana.

I can explain that.

Sana: No.

I seriously thought you gave a shit about me.

You actually REQUESTED him as a partner.

What are you trying to do?

Live out some middle school fantasy about hooking up with him?

It's actually sad.

I supported you.

I even understood when you weren't around to help me with college stuff and project stuff.

Because you were dealing with DNA stuff.

But knowing it was because you're trying to hook up with some guy who didn't even have time for you when he had a real girlfriend is pretty pathetic.

Me: Please stop.

Sana: And what about Iris?

Why didn't you ask her to help me?

Me: That was an honest mistake.

I forgot!

Sana: No. I'm mad.

You know what?

I've got my own email to forward you.

To: Cordelia Koenig (CordeliaBedelia99@gmail.com)
From: Sana Sasaki (sasakicentral@gmail.com)
Subject: Fwd: Re: Cordelia

Looks like I'm not the only one who is frustrated about the Cordelia Show.

To: Sana Sasaki (sasakicentral@gmail.com)
From: Bea Koenig (b.koenig@brown.edu)
Subject: Cordelia

Sana,

I haven't been able to get in touch with Cordelia for a while.

I'm sure you know better than anyone what's going on with her—unless she's alienated everyone but Kodiak. I should probably wait until I can get on the phone, but at this point I probably have a better chance of her calling me back if you pass the news on.

I know.

Last week, after we talked, I checked my GeneQuest account. I went into Settings and turned on the Connect option so I could add her as a relative—only the weirdest thing happened. It told me that she is my half sister. So yeah, I know. I've been trying to talk to her about it, but she won't answer any of my calls or texts—not that I blame her. I acted terrible when she tried talking to me about it. It's no wonder she's upset with me, but I'm starting to get worried, especially as I hear how awful she's doing.

I feel trapped. Like I have no choice but to talk to our parents. What do you think?

Bea

The following is a list of people I have lost the ability to text amid crisis in the past three weeks:

- Mom
- Dad
- Iris
- Sana
- Kodiak
- Jack

Sana-Friend ♥

Me: Please.
I feel like I have lost everything.
Sana: Go to bed. You're drunk.
Or call Bea.
She's dying to talk to you.

Sister-Bea

Me: Hey.

I just texted Sana.

I know you know.

I'm sorry.

Please message me back.

Bea: It's late.

Babe, get some rest.

We can talk tomorrow.

The following is a list of people I have lost the ability to text amid crisis in the past three weeks:

- Mom
- Dad
- Iris
- Sana
- Kodiak
- Jack
- Bea

I cry myself to sleep
on white hotel sheets
that smell like detergent
and sadness.

It feels like hugging a stranger
and waiting for them to suddenly
transform into a friend.

And then sleep takes me
like fog
settling over the mountains
frosting grass
to thaw
tomorrow.

I drag a fork through eggs,
squishing them against a plate
full of food
I'm too nauseated
to eat.

The lobby of people
filled with light
and no regret
about the things they did
and said
last night.

Kodiak sits on the other side
of the lobby
with his roommate,
sneaking glances at me.
He's a sad otter today,
bobbing
on the other side
of the ocean.

The sting of tears
reaches my eyes
when a hand drops
to my shoulder.

I look up
at Ms. Nadeer
and her inviting smile.
"Might I have a moment?"

"I've noticed a lot of changes in you this semester."
Ms. Nadeer sits,
looking over her shoulder
where Kodiak is pushing food
with his fork too.

"It's not him."
I sink lower in my chair.

"I know."
Her voice
is love—
"Your poems.
They aren't poems that ache from the heart
in the traditional sense—
but a matter of identity,
am I right?"

My bottom lip trembles,
shattering the mask
she can already see through.

"There was a time
after I'd graduated college.
I applied for a job
I really wanted

but was passed up.
Then another.
And another.

"I thought to myself,
what I was doing
wasn't working.
So I went back for grad school
and got my masters,
then realized my passions for helping
and teaching
and guidance.

"When something isn't working for you,
Cordelia,
you need to go back.
Find a way to better yourself.
Put wonderful things out in the world
and see if they help you find a path
More often than not,
if you are hung up on someone
or something
it isn't about them.
It's about you.

"Tell me.
Why did you come here?"
Ms. Nadeer sips
from a Styrofoam cup,
leaving berry-colored lipstick
on the rim.

"For the poetry conference."

Her smile says, *Okay*.
Her eyes say, *Try again*.

"To find part of myself."

"Well, have you?
Did you find yourself?"

"I think so.
I'm not sure
I like
what I found."
A single tear
slides down my cheek,
but there are
four billion more behind it.

"I've watched you these past weeks
trying on different hats.
And that's fine.
It's part of learning who you are.
But at the end of the day,
you have to be okay
with the you
inside your heart."

I'm struggling to think of something
anything
to say, when Ms. Nadeer fills the space
between us.
"You know,
it's not too late
to sign up for that poetry contest."

Ms. Nadeer points
to a white sign-up sheet
and smiles
as if she knows
that deep in my heart
my name is already on it.

I think back to
the Cordelia
before the truth.
And I remember
how she thought
she could coast
through this entire project
because poetry
was as much a part of her
as breathing.

A girl who wanted so badly
to see herself in her roots
and prove
once and for all
that she might fit somewhere.

How the bonus
of using the project as a chance
to listen
up close
to the boy who sings
his poems
was too much to pass up.

How she thought she
didn't have to work
at finding herself
because she already knew
who she was.

Early accepted
poet
dreamer
quiet muse
wonderer
friend
sister

daughter.

The truth changed so many things
My life
My view
My basic understanding of the world.
But it didn't change me.
Not really.
Not where it counts.

SIGN-UP SHEET
for
FOURTH ANNUAL
PACIFIC NORTHWEST YOUNG POETS
ASSOCIATION
Poetry Contest

Poems must be original work, performed by writer, and written in the last calendar year. A mandatory meeting will take place Sunday morning from 11:00 am–1:00 pm. If you are not there by 11:00 am, you forfeit your ability to participate.

Please sign up below. One entry per person.

I scrawl my name,
at the end of the page,
along with my grade
and school.

And when I step away,
I already feel
a little more
like me.

I turn to see Kodiak
staring at the floor,
reciting his poem.
When he finally looks up
at me
he doesn't smile
or nod,
but tightens his brows
jerking his head
in the other direction.
Kodiak's wings stay tucked close,
like he's afraid to fly.

I collect my things
and toss the food
I'm too hung over
to eat.
I can't help
the unshakable feeling
that someone
is still watching me.

I scan the cafeteria.
Nearly everyone
has drifted from the lobby
like an iceberg at sea.
There's a small group of women
laughing wildly in the corner,
but it's a man with a plaid shirt
near the hotel doors
who catches my eye.

It's unbuttoned in the front,
creating a V in the neckline
just enough
to reveal a tattoo
on his collarbone
of a woman
with devil horns.

From across the expanse of this lobby,
he is watching me,
running a hand through his hair
like he's afraid
to come talk to the girl
who shares his blood.

The girl he spun a tale to.
A snapshot of a foggy past,
an impossible future,
a lie I can't escape.
As he rubs the place
on the back of his head
where his motorcycle helmet
probably meets his neckline,
I want to scream.

To let every sound
I can make
explode from my mouth.
To let him hear
the invisible pain
he left in the wake
of his lies.
Promises
that were easy to make

because he never
had
to
make
them
true.

I take one step,
then another,
until I'm charging.
My feet slice me through
the thick air between us
like sleek hungry puffins
surging through arctic waters.

"It's you."
I almost exhale my words.

"Was it all a lie?"

"Most of it. Yeah."
I listen to his voice,
finding my reflection
in the single tear
on the rim of his eye.
"But the way I felt,
how much I wanted to know you,
that was all true."

I've been cut open
and spread out
so everyone can see
how every moment my heart pumps
is a moment it bleeds.
With my eyes tinged pink
and tears smeared down my face,
I shake my head
again
and
again
like if I do,
it'll wipe away
the past weeks
as a false memory.

"Why?"
I scream the poison,
leeching the infection
from my shaking body

"I didn't want you to think
I'm the loser
your mom remembers."

At last
the dam
has broken.
This picture
made real.
His eyes
his voice
telling me what I already knew
but desperately hoped wasn't true.
I stand there,
crying.
While Jack doesn't say
a word.

Because there's no place
or time
where I fit
in his life.

Because it wouldn't have only been a lie
about who he was.
It would have been
a lie about coming to a school play
a lie about visiting every other holiday
a lie about a late Christmas card
lost in the mail.

And I finally see
how my mom
wanted so badly
to believe the lie.

I don't know what to say
because my mind
has departed

Like I'm circling the lobby
above my head
spinning
spiraling
a seedpod with perfect fins
twirling in the gust
of a cold autumn wind.

My ears are ringing
and my eyes are as heavy
as three feet of snow
fallen in one night.

His face looks like mine
but older
and sadder,
a story that belongs to a stranger.

I feel a hand slip around mine,
and at first
I think it's Jack
reaching for me.

But as I look down,
it's Kodiak's hand.
I can't see what he's doing,
but I can feel the heart he's drawing in my palm.

Kodiak's face has the story of a stranger.
It says, *We have to go*.
And he looks at me
like he really sees me.
Like there's never been
a picture
where the two of us
don't belong together.

I turn to Jack,
~~not~~ my father
a crumbling paradox
I wanted
more than anything
to be real.
I turn toward the safe place
he never was.

"I have to go—
I have this poetry thing
and it starts in a few minutes."

"Oh."
Jack gasps the word
like a memory has suddenly caught flame.
His voice
wraps around the word,
a tender squeeze.

"Poetry.
Your mom loved poetry too."

How
do I say goodbye
when this never
felt
like hello?

How do I say goodbye to a lie?
How do I let go of wondering
and wishing
and hoping
the truth
is something
it's not?

How do I let go of the lie
that is me?

Walking away,
like I know I should.
Stepping out of the path
of heartache,
I look over my shoulder
where Jack stares on,
stunned.

I call back,
"There's a presentation
in the lobby
around six.
If.
You want to come."

My steps fall into rhythm
with Kodiak's.
Together,
but I'm one beat
behind.

Kodiak keeps glancing at me
while I look at my feet,
aching
to go back
to my room
and cry
into my sheets
that smell like
detergent.

I tell him,
"Thank you,"
but I don't look up
because his brown eyes
might swallow me whole
if I let myself
see him this close
after last night.
"You didn't have to come over there."

"That had to be hard."
He stops,
grabbing both my hands
to force my blurry
gaze to his.
"It's not something
anyone
should have to go through
alone."

"I wanted this."
I let our hands fall limp
between us
before I leave him.
Away from this.
Away from everything.

Sana-Friend ♥

Me: Okay.

I'm supposed to be paying attention at this meeting.

But I can't.

Remember that time I got really mad you?

When you told your mom I wanted to try out for

cheerleading?

And then she told my mom.

Who went all crazy and tried to coach me?

Remember how mad I was?

I forgave you.

Sana: That doesn't

remotely

sound like an apology.

Or even remotely close to the same thing.

I'm still not talking to you.

Me: Please?

Jack showed up at the hotel.

Sana: Well fucksticks.

Ceasefire.

What the hell?

Are you okay?

Me: No.

I don't know.

I can't think right now.

I'm shaking so bad I can barely see my phone.

Sana: Is Kodi there?

Me: You're calling him Kodi now?

I knew I didn't tell him where Jack lives!

How many emails did you exchange about me?

Sana: Enough to tell him I was worried about you.

Is he there?

Me: Kinda.

It's weird.

Last night some stuff happened with him.

And I can't even look at him.

Sana: Wait.

So many freaking questions.

One thing at a time.

What was Jack like?

As hot as he is on Instagram?

Me: Ew!

That is so gross.

He was . . .

Sad.

Sana: You must get that from him.

Me: I must.

But you were right.

Basically everything he ever told me was a huge lie.

Sana: Damn.

Me: I'm sorry.

I owe you.

When I get home, I'll help you with whatever you need.

Sana: Too bad.

Emma fucking Daniels is helping now.

She's a wizard with a camera and has some really killer makeup tutorials.

And BONUS: turns out YouTube is a soccer lesson mecca.

Me: I'm really sorry.

I should have requested you.

I'm an ass.

This whole project was a mistake.

Sana: Yeah.

You should have.

But it's working out fine.

I was going to have to figure out how to do life without your constant supervision next year anyway.

Speaking of mistakes.

What exactly happened with Kodiak last night?

Me: Oh man.

I don't think I can talk about it yet.

I doubt you want to hear any more about that saga anyway.

Let's just say I don't think I'll ever be able to look at him again.

Sana: That effing ass.

Tell me now.

Or the ceasefire is unceased.

Me: Okay.

So last night he took me to a bar so I could try to find Jack.

Spoiler alert: I didn't.

But I was upset.

And somehow we ended up back in his hotel room drinking.

Sana: Okay I don't like where this is going.

Me: One thing led to another.

And we ended up half-naked on the bed.

Then I told him I was ready.

Sana: HOLY SHIT.

You HAVE changed.

So what did he do?

Me: I really don't want to even talk about this.

Sana: I'm going to kill him.

Aren't I?

What I wouldn't give to be able to cash in cigarettes for air miles.

Come there.

And kick his ass.

I can't believe your first time was with Kodiak Jones.

Are you okay?

Me: No.

But we didn't have sex.

Sana: Wait what?

Me: I wanted to.

I tried.

Basically threw myself at him.

And he turned me down.

This is so embarrassing.

Sana: Sorry.

But I'm really fucking confused now.

So you took off all your clothes.

While drunk.

And you're upset that he respected the fact you were

not in a position to consent?

Me: When you put it that way . . .

It doesn't sound as bad.

Sana: Because it's not.

He did you good here.

Well

I mean, he didn't actually do you at all.

But he was a solid guy.

Me: You're not helping my embarrassment.

Sana: Listen.

I know I'm not the biggest Cordiak fan.

But that's mostly because I think you've been

holding on to a version of him that doesn't exist anymore.

But you obviously see something in him

everyone else doesn't.

He's there for you.

He's been there for you.

Go talk to him.

Write him a poem.

Do whatever it is you writer weirdos do.

When Kodiak Jones
writes his poems,
it's like his whole world
bleeds into verse
on paper.
Like his soul
and his ancestor's souls
bleed
into poetry.

When Kodiak Jones
plays guitar
and sings you back
the words you've written,
you start to think
he sees inside you.

That your heart and his
have met before
in another picture
making harmonious music
bleeding magnificent verse
telling ghost stories
and howling like wolves.

When Kodiak Jones
traces a heart in your hand,
it's because he knows you need it.
That's who he is.
The one who helps when it hurts him.
The one who doesn't know it's okay
to leave behind the broken ones
to make room for himself.

I'm the only iceberg in the world
who calved from her glacier,
went out into the ocean,
but then tethered herself back
to the glacier
she should have never left.

Kodiak Jones

Me: Hey.

Kodiak: You're right in front of me.

You can just turn around and talk to me you know.

Me: I know.

But it'd be weird.

There's a bunch of people around.

And we're all about to go on stage.

Kodiak: Yeah.

Me: I'm sorry.

About last night.

And the night before.

I'm sorry about all of it.

Kodiak: Please don't apologize.

Delia.

I don't ever want you to apologize about last night.

Or the night before.

Me: You were being a good guy.

I felt rejected.

I care so much about you.

Kodiak: I care so much about you too.

Me: But I have to be honest with myself.

My reasons for liking you were made up in my head

before we knew each other like that.

About your writing.

And what my perception of you was based on what you
were like when we were kids.

Kodiak: Oh.

Me: The truth is you're so much better than the version
in my head.

The boy who sings his poems.

And opens his whole body up when he speaks about
writing.

And before you go up there

and bare your soul

for sport,

I want you to know you're amazing.

I don't deserve the friend you've been to me.

Right before he goes on,
Kodiak paces
behind the stage curtain.

I sneak next to him,
reach for his hand,
and draw a heart on his palm.

When his name is called,
he smiles,
kisses me on the cheek,
and disappears onto the stage.

There is a boy,
who held my hand
through the hardest moment
of my life.

And I never saw
he was hurting too
until he sang his poem
on a stage
in front of people
about being a sad raven
crying for the love
of a shiny treasure
he never got to hold.

And I watched,
from the sidelines,
as his body folded in,
and the color sprang from his mouth
and he gave every
person
in the audience
an iridescent glimpse
of his pain.

His promise
to a girl
about a baby.

The picture he painted himself in
washed away
before his very eyes
while he struggled
between relief and fear,
guilt and shame.

Sadness for what was washed away
and hope for the fresh canvas.

After Kodiak.
And a guy from Seattle,
a girl from Bellingham,
and another from Oregon somewhere.

My name
is called.
Kodiak smiles down at me,
the memory of his treasure
still staining his smile.
He leans in, whispers to me,
"Go out there
and show off
what's in that heart of yours."

I should be nervous,
but a cool chill
settles over me,
as I step out on the stage.
And realize
saying my words
doesn't scare me
as much as
seeing Jack
in the crowd would.

I think about the mountains
close to home where my real dad is.
And how the deep grooves
carved by forgotten snow
are home to
bears
rabbits
moose
berries
even me.

How after this,
I get to go back.

I push Jack out of my mind,
and walk on
to recite a poem
for a man
who probably won't be there.

I'm ten steps away
from the stage,
with complete
silence
from the crowd.

My peers,
I have barely
gotten to know,
because I was too busy
getting to know myself.

And I realize,
of all the people in the world,
I want him here.
The guy who started this all.
Because this poem,
this journey,
wouldn't be anything

if it didn't start with
the man I came
to meet.

My father.

I smooth my poem down on the podium,
even though I know it by heart.
It sits in my memory
like all of Kodiak's songs
and Sana's laugh
and Dad's Shakespeare quotes
and Mom's hugs
and Iris's hashtags
and even Bea's snark.

It's not hard to memorize
the thing
that touches
your soul.

Both hands
at my sides,
I let myself
look for him.

Scanning the crowd,
hoping that after all this:
the flight
the heartbreak
of learning
who he really is—

he finally stepped up
and decided
to be a father.
My father.

Just for today.

I hope
with every ounce
I have left
he doesn't let me down.
I close my eyes,
wishing
for the impossible.

I want my father here.
Please,
just this once,
be here.
Please, don't let me down.

When I open my eyes
the lights are brighter somehow
and they shift my focus,
settling on a face
I know.

My heart
races.
It's in a sprint
as it tries
to keep up with my mind.
My stomach churning
like pebbles
rolling along a riverbed.

Standing
almost directly in front of me,
in the center of the crowd
is my father.

My Shakespeare-loving,
quoting,
joking

father.

Standing next to him,
my mom curls her arm around his.
Iris
waving like she's eight instead of twelve.
Even Bea flew out from school,
but she's too cool to wave.
We'll talk tomorrow.
She gives me a nod, a small smile
that tells me we're okay.

They stand there,
supporting me
even when I didn't ask for it.

I want to bask in the weightless
happiness
radiating through my chest,
but it's something else
that creeps in.
A tightness,
a suffocation
trapped beneath ice.

Jack.
Ten or so feet away
from my exit.

I draw in
the length
of my breath,
remembering the first message
Jack sent me.
My first hint
of the first lie
that led to my life.

But then I see my parents.
I exhale.
I imagine crushing up that message
and throwing it in the trash.

Because what I feel now
isn't the weight of sadness
or fear I don't belong
in this picture.

It's happiness so brittle
it shatters into relief,
knowing I have a place
in the picture of my family
forever.

I look to my mother
while I try to forget
Jack is lingering near the exit door.
Attempting to tell her with my eyes
what I'm about to read
was never meant for her to hear.

And as if she hears everything,
as if her heart knows mine,
she nods.

The Truth Project
by Cordelia Koenig

They say
nature brought you into this world.
But what if my roots
have grown around lies?
What if they're coiled around a promise
two people made
but could not keep?

What if nature is just a way
to blame your problems
on what should have been?
Like my leaves
should be evergreen
because my father's
are evergreen.
Why are mine
stained the color of tangerines?

Then my leaves fall,
scattering to the ground
like confetti celebrating the end of summer.
My father's stay green.

And when winter's frost sets in—
my branches bitter cold
and covered in snow.
I wonder if I will ever grow leaves again
or if they have disappeared
because I have also disappeared.

But then something magical happens.
After I've dusted off winter's frost
and seen how fall's leaves have helped me grow,
I can look beyond the nature of my foliage
to the roots that nurtured me.

And roots,
no matter what decorate the branches,
stretch out beneath the ground
—intertwined with other trees
that might not look the same
but have identical systems of growth.

Turn instead to what has always been.
Crawl into the shade of the trees that protect you,
collapse beneath the canopy
of what you know is true.

Feel how you are loved
and love them back.

After the performance,
when my hands have stopped shaking
and I can no longer hear the sound
of my heart
in my ears—
I'm escorted off the stage
to my family.

Weaving through a crowd of people
I find the ones that belong to me
in place of the one that never did.

Iris gets to me first,
wrapping me in a hug,
saying,
"I want to be a poet too."

Bea waves from next to our parents
in that way that is familiar
and removed.
But she's got tears in her eyes
that say she's a little proud.

Mom is a mess,
her face
blotchy

and her
mouth
pulled back over her teeth.
I can't tell if she's sobbing
or smiling.

Dad pulls me in
for a hug
and I accept the promise
that almost wasn't.
The scents of his teaching-shirt,
like paper
and books
and history.
His laugh.
While he rubs my hair
and leans into my ear
and whispers.
"A hit.
A very palpable hit."

Over his shoulder,
I watch as Jack ruffles a hand through his hair,
smiling through stranger eyes,
like he might like the view he has.

Me.

Happy.

With my family.

"Why are you here?
I ask.
"I told you I wasn't going to be performing."

 "We thought"
—Mom smiles,
in a slow careful way—
"you might want us here."
Dad adds,
"We thought you might need us."

When it's just me
and Dad,
because everyone else
has gone for drinks
and snacks,
I look over my shoulder
scanning
everyone's families
for the eyes of a man
who is more broken
than me.

"Honey,
who are you looking for?"
Dad asks.

I lie:
"Kodiak,"
and I point to the place
where he's sitting,
laughing with his friends
like his wings
have been freed
and he can finally fly again.

Dad tilts his chin down,
all sympathy and love.
But shakes his head
softly with knowing.

"Are you going to stick with that answer,
my sweet, sweet Cordelia?
Because I think you're looking for Jack."

There's something in me
that breaks
while his jade eyes
are drawn to mine.
As if we've had this secret
all along.
"I saw him leave a few minutes ago."

I throw my arms around his neck,
the way I did the night he picked me up
from Fletcher's.
And when I've finally got all the courage
I can muster,
I ask my father
how he knew
I was looking for the man
he's not supposed to know about.

"I'm your dad—"
his voice is trembling as he speaks.
"I watched you come into this world
red faced and screaming.
I held your hand
when you tumbled into your first steps
the way you've tumbled through life:
headfirst.

I'm the one who was there when you
went off to kindergarten
and told us you couldn't go back
because they didn't teach you anything
but letters—
and you already knew those.

I'm the one who's always been here, Delia.
I've been watching you hurt
these past few weeks.
Trying to find yourself
in something that wasn't there.
Of course I knew."

"But Mom said . . ."

"That's a conversation for another time.
Your mother and I
had to have a lot of tough conversations
after you took that test.
Ones we've needed to have for a long time.
But I'll tell you this:
I've known
since before you were born,
and it didn't change anything for me.
'I love you more than words can wield the matter;
Dearer than eye-sight,
space,
and liberty.
Beyond what can be valued.'
I am proud to call you my daughter.
I am proud to be your dad.

No one
can change that."

Mom comes back
without my sisters.
She loops her arms around me.
She whispers words that feel like
An Alaskan sunset at
two in the morning,
the ocean breeze in your face.
Like home.

"I'm sorry."

And my heart is so full
and my mind is so free.
I don't think I'll ever
feel this whole again.

Over the loudspeaker
a crackled voice announces
they're ready to conclude
the weekend
by celebrating winners
of the poetry contest.

All around us
my friends
teachers
and family
gather.
Mom squeezes my hand,
and two rows up
I see Kodiak throw a thumbs-up in my direction,
mouthing *Good luck*.
Mom whispers something about knowing
I'll win,
for sure.

But I don't care if my name is called
or not,
because I look at my dad,
my real dad,
and realize
I've already won.

"And the winner of this year's
Young Poet Award
for the Pacific Northwest Young Poets Association
Contest
comes all the way from Tundra Cove, Alaska."

Dad reaches for my hand,
grabbing it tight
like it might make them
call my name.

"Kodiak Jones
for his poem
'RAVEN'!"

Ms. Nadeer is the first to shout,
standing in her seat,
yelling
like it was her words
that won.

I jump up too,
and when Kodiak reaches the stage,
head in his hands,
unable to say anything—
every other student from Tundra Cove

joins him.
Wrapping him up
in all the love
they can
for a boy
whose trouble
feels a little lighter today.

Mom looks over at me,
brushing away happy tears,
and smiles.
"Go."

I'm the last one
to the stage,
and when I finally reach him,
Kodiak pulls me close.

His dark eyes don't threaten
to swallow me whole
the way they used to.
He's not so untouchable
these days.
The boy whose heart
I thought I already knew,
and whose heart I want to
get to know again.

Sometimes you can say everything you need to say
with a single look.
Something like:

I'm sorry I wasn't there for you when you needed me.
I'm sorry I took up all the space
for my own hurt when you were hurting too.
I'm sorry things aren't going to be the same,
but maybe
that's okay
too.

I feel his kiss coming
the same way I feel the ocean
tickle my toes
before a wave.

We kiss,
and it's like
no one else
is here.
Even with the cheer
and chaos around us
and my parents in the crowd
and everyone so close—
It's only us

basking in the heat
of our own story,
writing our own song,
playing our own music,
projecting our own truth.

Jack Bisset

Jack: I'm sorry I didn't stay. But when your parents showed up I figured I shouldn't stick around. I heard your poem. It was beautiful, and you're really talented, I wish I could say that was because of me. Seeing you happy with your dad and even your mom made me realize maybe everything happened the way it did for a reason.
Me: Thank you. I think so too.
Jack: Maybe someday down the line we can talk again? I promise I'll be honest next time.
Me: I think I'd like that.

ONE MONTH LATER

Sana-Friend ♥

Me: Did you change your status to "It's complicated" on
Facebook?

Sana: Mayyyyyyybe.

Dude.

Where are you?

Emma and I have been waiting at your locker.

FOREEEEEEVER.

Me: Outside Ms. Nadeer's office.

Going to turn in my senior project.

Tell Emma hi!!!

Sana: Finally!

Maybe if you weren't busy sucking face with Kodiak

ALL THE EFFING TIME

you'd have had it finished sooner.

Me: Have you even turned yours in yet?

Maybe if you weren't sucking face with Emma

ALL THE FREAKING TIME

you'd have finished YOURS sooner.

Sana: Erroneous.

Me: Someone's been studying her SAT words.

Sana: No I'm not done.

I'm busy being a YouTube Star.

Did I tell you a scout for the University of Denver saw
my video and wants to chat scholarships?

Me: Only three times.

Today.

About ten yesterday.

Sana: Looks like I might go to Denver after all!

And without your help might I add!

Me: Okay. Ms. Nadeer's last student is leaving.

I gotta go!

"Please, Cordelia, sit!"
Ms. Nadeer points toward the chair.
I push my project
typed and stapled,
hidden in a manila folder,
toward her.

The poems I've worked on all spring
so personal
so private
I had no intention of ever using them
for this project.

"You worked harder than almost any other student
to find yourself this year.
It's admirable."
Her voice soars
like she's in the clouds
just looking at me.
"What is it that you learned?"

I smile.
I've thought a lot about this.
How my question this year was to understand
how ancestry shapes me.

I think ancestry only shapes you
if you want it to.

How you can go your whole life
never knowing what you were meant to be
and never knowing what you could have been
and still
be you.

How family
is the thing that shapes you.
The nurturing from the people closest to you
and the experiences you share
are the things that make you whole.

I learned,
through this project,
that the man who contributed to my DNA
isn't the one who made me who I am.
That was the man who raised me,
who watched my first steps,
and encouraged me every step after—
even when it took me away from him.

I shrug,
a shrug that almost hurts,

diminishing the last few months
to an essay question.

"Nothing I didn't already know,
deep down."

ACKNOWLEDGMENTS

First and foremost, thank you Reader. The fact that you chose to read my words means everything to me.

To Talon, my Tlingit Lovebird, without your help and sacrifice I wouldn't have been able to write this book or any book. Thank you for the late-night conversations where we get to share our worlds. *Ich liebe dich.* To my daughters for inspiring me. I hope one day you follow your dreams too. You are my world.

To my sisters (in all forms) for being my first readers. Beth, Crystal, Danae, Caprice: your cheerleading kept me going past that very first rough draft of that very first book. To my parents (Dad, Mom, etc.) for giving me all sorts of crazy things to write about ;) and my parents-in-law (Dawn and Max) for the support in babysitting during conferences and retreats and Diane Walter for the same. Kali and Rajessica, for constant and unequivocal support amid your own chaotic lives. And to Amy Wamy, my very own Sana—thank you for reading the whole thing out loud with me and whispering "it's so good" after every part.

My family at The Bent Agency: Louise Fury, agent extraordinaire, thank you for seeing something in this story and me. Molly Ker Hawn for passing my manuscript to Louise. Amelia Hodgson, thanks for all that you do. Jenny, Victoria, and the rest of The Bent Agency team—your support through this entire adventure has meant the world to me. And a very special thanks to Kristin Smith for believing in this book.

To everyone at HarperTeen and Quill Tree Books: Rosemary Brosnan and Jessica MacLeish for believing in this book enough to acquire it. Jessica, hearing you talk about Cordelia like she was an actual person was unforgettable. Alyssa Miele, thank you for helping me breathe even more life into Cordelia and the rest of my characters. And for following me down many an enneagram wormhole. Jon Howard and Robin Roy, thank you for making sure *The Truth Project* was as polished as could be. To the design team: Erin Fitzsimmons, Amy Ryan, and Lisa Vega—you helped make magic out of my words. And Emma Leonard for the stunning artwork—the first piece of the story people see. And a very special thanks to the marketing team.

To my Alaska writing friends: Alaska Writers Guild for being my home. Stefanie Tatalias and the rest of the crew at SCBWI Alaska for all your support. To everyone at The Writers Block for the good coffee and delicious food to draft with. Brooke Hartman, thank you for tearing up the rough draft's intro page. 1) you were right and 2) I'll never say that again. Marc Cameron (or is it Tom Clancy? I can never remember) for that incredible pep talk at the conference. Sarah Squared: I love our Sunday Squad. You both keep me excited to write.

Clelia Gore and Jessica Faust: for being there that first night and crying with me over a glass of Spenard Roadhouse's finest champagne. Jessica Grace Kelly (who, it should be known, was Kodiak Jones's first fan) for sharing so much of yourself so I *could* write this story. Scott and Jeremy (and Harvey and Archie) for giving me a place to write and being my Seattle on-the-ground research team. Katie and Sylvia, thank you for being here for every step of this journey.

And to my closest writing partners without whose constant hand holding I would not have been able to write any of this book: Deborah Maroulis, for being the last person between me and my first query, the 1 to my 7. Thank you for pushing me to make the jump. Vanessa Torres, for never letting me get away with anything, and always following plot bunnies with me—and for your writing-retreat Elmo impersonations. Lindsay Pierce, my BB4L and sometimes therapist. Thanks for letting me sit next to you at PNWA all those years ago. Who knew it would come to all this? Thank you for being a part of this journey and always telling me how proud you are of me.

My writing community, all my fellow 20's debuts: I LOVE YOU ALL.